देशी dharma aur dilemma

INDICA

desi dharma aur dilemma

BEYOND MOVIES, MUSIC, MUFTI AND MASALA

RAJESH SENGAMEDU

INDICA

Copyright © Rajesh Sengamedu 2024
All Rights Reserved.

ISBN

Hardcase 979-8-89673-428-4
Paperback 979-8-89673-426-0

Contents

Preface by Dr. Prasad Kaipa

Navigating *Dharma* in a Changing World

Over twenty-five years ago, I met Rajesh Sengamedu at a workshop I conducted in Bangalore. Even then, Rajesh struck me as someone with a profound curiosity and an eagerness to understand both himself and the larger cultural dynamics that shape us. In the decades that followed, our paths diverged and crossed again, and I found him to have grown into a reflective thinker and a successful executive, adept at balancing his Western influences and Indian roots. This book, *Desi Dharma aur Dilemma*, embodies Rajesh's journey and his keen observations about what it means to be both rooted and adaptive, holding on to cultural essence while living far from its physical soil. I am impressed that he can write in a way that he connects with both youth, their parents and their mindsets.

Rajesh brings together a collection of stories that reflect the modern-day dilemmas faced by both Indian immigrants in the West and youth in India. These stories resonate deeply with both audiences, as they navigate issues of identity, belonging, and cultural integration. These are dilemmas of identity, culture, and belonging: questions that I see many youth, whether they are children of Indian Americans or youth in India, are struggling with today. How do we hold on to traditions without being rigid? How do we integrate into a new world without losing our essence? Rajesh illustrates these challenges vividly through relatable stories that seamlessly transition from the specific to the universal, drawing us into their deeper significance.

One such story that stood out to me is titled *"Saptapadi Saat Samundar Paar."* It reflects the struggle of a young couple—Ravi, a first-generation Indian American, and Mei, his partner—as they grapple with what marriage truly means. For Ravi's parents, marriage is anchored in the *Saptapadi* (seven sacred steps around fire) that signify a lifelong commitment beyond just emotional companionship. But for Ravi, raised amidst Western ideals of individual freedom and experimentation, the idea of commitment feels negotiable, as if it can be deferred until a more convenient time. Rajesh captures this tension beautifully, highlighting both the parents' heartfelt yearning to preserve something sacred and Ravi's genuine confusion in a world that doesn't always assign value to traditional rites. This story reflects the current dynamics faced by many young Indian Americans and Indian youth alike, where family expectations intersect with personal autonomy, leaving both parents and children to navigate an evolving understanding of tradition and modern relationships. For parents, this story also offers insights into the internal conflicts that the youth of today experience, shedding light on the complexity behind decisions that may appear simple on the surface.

Another poignant narrative in the book, "Bigoted Boss," portrays the workplace struggles of Ramana, a devout Hindu, who finds himself targeted by his boss for wearing sacred ash (*vibhuti*) on his forehead during a Zoom meeting.

In a professional setting that prides itself on diversity, Ramana's expression of faith suddenly becomes a point of contention. Rajesh uses this story to examine the ironies of modern corporate culture—spaces that strive for inclusivity yet often dismiss expressions of cultural or religious identity that do not fit into mainstream Western norms. This narrative reminds us of the nuanced negotiations many Indian Americans must undertake daily, balancing the desire to stay true to their roots with the practical need to fit in professionally. It speaks to the quiet, often invisible challenges of being authentic in environments that may feel subtly, or overtly, exclusionary.

The dilemmas Rajesh writes about are the dilemmas faced by today's children of Indian immigrants as well as youth in India—those who live with one foot firmly planted in the soil of their ancestral culture while the other ventures into the often conflicting landscape of Western ideals. These stories offer valuable lessons for both groups and can also be eye-opening for parents who want to understand the nuanced challenges their children are navigating. These stories reveal the quiet, often invisible struggles these young people face balancing expectations at home with societal pressures outside, making sense of cultural practices that may not come with ready explanations, and deciding which parts of their heritage they will carry forward or let go of. For example, the practice of rituals like *Sandhyavandanam* or traditional marriage customs can often feel out of place in a Western setting, yet their deeper meanings can offer grounding in times of uncertainty. As someone who has moved between India and the United

States, I see the universality of these experiences and how they resonate deeply with the children of so many Indian American families today.

What makes *Desi Dharma aur Dilemma* so compelling is Rajesh's refusal to offer neat solutions. Instead, he encourages us to sit with the ambiguity—to recognize that Dharma is not about rigid right or wrong but about context, discernment, and what serves the greater good. This is particularly well-expressed in several stories which resonate deeply not only with youth but also provide parents with a window into the dilemmas faced by the younger generation.

For parents like me, who watch their children navigate these challenges, and for young Indian Americans who are forging their own path, Rajesh offers not so much a guide as a mirror—a way to understand that these struggles are part of a long lineage of questions, and that finding one's path is itself an act of living one's Dharma. Embracing this ambiguity, as Rajesh shows, is not a weakness but a profound strength that allows us to adapt without losing ourselves.

I hope this book sparks the same reflection and dialogue that I have enjoyed in my conversations with Rajesh over the years. His stories remind us that growth, understanding, and compassion are often found in embracing our dilemmas rather than wishing them away. As you read, I encourage you to discuss these stories with your families and peers—may this work offer insight, comfort, and perhaps even inspiration to both youth and parents who find themselves navigating the dual worlds of tradition and modernity, East and West.

For parents, these stories serve as an invitation to better understand the complexities their children face, encouraging empathy and open dialogue.

– Dr. Prasad Kaipa,
San Jose, November 2024
Co-author of bestseller: From Smart to Wise: Acting and
Leading with Wisdom
Co-founder, Institute of Indic Wisdom,
Board Member, Retired CEO Coach and Advisor
https://www.linkedin.com/in/prasadkaipa/

Dharma

धारयति इति धर्मः

That which protects (all beings) is *dharma*

***

Dilemma

A difficult situation where a choice must be made

Why You Should Read This Book?

Let me explain with a metaphor.

Imagine you are all alone in a deep jungle, standing on the banks of a very powerful river, whose flow you cannot control or stop in any way. In the river, unbeknown to you, there will be sudden rapids, big sharp rocks. A little afar downstream, this river is going to soon become a giant waterfall. The fall from there will be fatal. There are other unknown dangers in the water too.

Sadly, you don't know any of these dangers or the fatal waterfall.

Your friend is waiting for you on the other side. He has a jeep to take you out to safety from that jungle. All you wanted to do was to cross the river to meet him.

What would you do?

Yes, you will first examine the river. Perhaps go up and down the river to assess and then finally chose a vantage point from where you will swim upstream to compensate for the water flow so that you don't go down the waterfall.

Then take the plunge and swim. Once in the waters, you also navigate other dangers that come along, and your key strategy is to avoid that waterfall at all costs.

Finally, imagine the difficulty if you did not know how to swim.

Your friend with the jeep is your goal post in life.

The lonely jungle are the distant shores that *desis* are living today.

The flowing river represents the various influences – false narratives, indoctrination and brainwashing – wokeism, radical religious conversions, pseudo-secularism, racism, sophisticated manipulation to name a few – that you or your 'atomic' family members – your children especially, will encounter, just trying to adapt and live in a new environment. Sadly, it also includes our own ignorance, misunderstanding, wrong conclusions and beliefs. The influences are not always known to you unfortunately.

The waterfall represents the deep abyss, confusion, frustration, depression and lost years of happiness, contentment & peace.

Being alone should be nothing new to anyone living in US. Already the migrant families are nuclear families. They are rapidly becoming atomic and individualistic with friends as the best support system, instead of joint family, extended family & friend systems that we found in India a generation ago. Being alone also leads soon to loneliness in most people, reducing their defenses, and lowering their immunity, allowing the influences to easily enter and corrupt the mind.

Swimming represents your anchor in, and deep understanding of a strong, unshakeable foundation. It helps you and your atomic family members to navigate the strong influences with dexterity and confidence towards your goal. It helps you to make rational, pre-meditated logical choices to avoid the danger of being washed away.

In the US, there are several stories of people going through situations that shake their very core. One needs to just look around carefully within their own friend & family circle and research a bit more on Internet to know.

The **words of *Pujya Swami* Dayananda Saraswati**[1], explains the current Hindu mind very well:

Bharat is politically free today, but her soul is in chains. What we now adore and follow as our heritage are some pithless ethics, effete customs and worn-out formulas. Our conception of culture does not extend beyond theatres and dance drama festivals. These and many similar things are our heritage today and it is under the stranglehold of this heritage, the soul of Bharat wails, softly and ceaselessly.

Menace to our Dharma did not come so much from the crusaders of alien faiths as it came from our own people. If we are to convert the Hindus into true Hinduism, we should help them first rise above these negatives of bigotry and sectarianism. For this they are to be educated – educated thoroughly in their scriptures like Gita and Upanishads.

In addition, the current education system and lifestyle, particularly in the urban areas, create minds that are

---

1   Paraphrased for brevity

neutralized. These people remain unaware of the depth of Vedic tradition and dharma they are born in, and who are inheritors of a cultural wealth that could be the envy of the world. Yet they are reluctant, even embarrassed to discuss their culture or religion.

Some of the stories you are about to read, are commonplace stories that can happen anywhere, for various reasons, like work related stress. The silent virus though is the various influences that people succumb to, even without knowing that they are being indoctrinated. This stems from ignorance of one's own rich foundations or disdain towards own culture. It also can stem from 'pseudo-secular' indoctrination from our childhood.

Like what happens to the protagonist of the movie, **The Kerala Story**. Although some facts are yet to be verified, no one can question the indoctrination and her consequent downfall. If it can happen in a milieu that had strong family and society support in India, worse can happen in the far shores overseas where we lack the the societal and familial support system.

There are stories of real people in the US, where children have misunderstood the *Varna* system and campaigned actively against their own self-interest, which is likely to have imported the 'caste' system into what is primarily a meritocracy-based culture in US.

There are also stories of real people who got swayed away by radical theology and convert to another religion, only to feel stuck in it and guilty. They also leave behind broken families divided by religion.

Finally, there are stories of children who grow up confused in the US, even about basic facts like sex/gender, or have been taught wrongly about their own Hindu culture. These children grow up to be radical rebels rejecting their own culture, with their own inherent negative unsubstantiated biases.

Desi Dharma aur Dilemma is a book of my musings and observations, focused on *Hindus*. My focus is to highlight misunderstandings about *Sanatana Dharma* and the perilous effects this has on individuals and families. Sometimes, the effects lasting multiple generations.

Most of the stories are just narration of dilemmas I observed. These anonymized stories are what I know of directly, as well as some that I researched on the Internet. Reddit was a great source of dilemmas that *Desis* faced. Some of my friends shared their ideas too. I added *masala* on top of the basic themes. I also took help from Gemini, ChatGPT & Claude to embellish and edit these stories.

Typically, written up like a short conversation or two between friends, where they discuss and debate their ideas about a situation and how they think about it. I don't want to make any moral judgement on their decisions. I chose to leave them inconclusive by design most of the times.

I tried my best to be non-judgmental and left the stories inconclusive where possible. Through these stories, my goal is to raise the *desi* curiosity to go deeper to understand the philosophy. When we go beyond the mere visible appearances of our culture in the form of Movies, Music, *Mufti* (clothes) and *Masala* (food) and understand the 'why' underneath, culture becomes an active verb to guide us in our *dharma* to resolve our dilemma.

But what is *dharma?*

Dharma

Preparations for the inevitable battle are going on in the Kaurava camp. After having spent thirteen years in the tough forests, the Pandavas wanted their kingdom back as was promised during the fateful game of dice. Sanjaya, the emissary of King Dhritarashtra comes from Hastinapura with an overture of peace.

At the brink of the war, Duryodhana was mighty pleased to have secured the entire Yadava army, leaving for Arjuna, the magician Krishna, who would vow not to lift any weapon. Immense destruction was imminent. Loss of life, property, and subsequent degradation of the society.

Yudhishtira knows the outcomes. The loser will lose everything in this war. And the winner is a loser too. That's when he, the eldest of the Pandavas whose immense strength was always his wisdom and actions always directed to protect *dharma*, turns to Krishna for advice[2]:

---

2   यदि ह्यहम् विसृजन् साम गर्ह्यो नियुध्यमानो यदि जह्याम् स्वधर्मम् ।
महायशा: केशवस्तद् ब्रवितु वासुदेवस्तूभयोरर्थकाम: ॥

      – महाभारते उद्योग पर्व २८.१०

Whether giving up the kingdom, I would be blameless, or if by fighting I would abandon *dharma*, let Lord Krishna decide. Krishna seeks welfare for both (Kauravas and Pandavas).

      – Mahabharata, Udyoga Parva 28.10

They say, Mahabharata is all about *Dharma*. And even *Dharmaputra* Yudhishtira, the son of the very embodiment of *Dharma* principle needed advice. To fight or not to fight. His younger brother and the valiant Arjuna would face the same conundrum on the first day of the battlefield.

Dharma can be an elusive concept. It is elusive even today, not just in the days of Mahabharata. It is very easy to mistake it and assign false equivalence that it is the laws of the country. It is simple to understand yet complex to encode it in laws and there is always a difficulty to apply practically. If it is a law to drive on the right of the road in US, it is illegal in UK or India. If capital punishment is banned in a country, it is OK in another. We can give numerous examples like this. *Dharma* is not geography bound, country bound or time bound. It is eternal.

Dharma is the very nature of a being, thing, or the elements.

Innumerable doubts come to our mind as to what is right and what is wrong. Moreover, we have our own conception of morality and personal ethics. Some of us, thanks to the gift of Lord Macaulay and the British, and unknowingly and inadvertently are schooled in ethics borrowed from rigid principles from other religions. Which may or may not be aligned to what truly is *dharma* in that situation.

Dharma is not ethics, morals, or values. Those are woefully inadequate translations in English. *Dharma* should be understood from the source, the way it is. However, we ended up learning and interpreting our culture from a Western lens. It was the lens of Abrahamic religions.

Dharma is neither static nor can be engraved in stone. There are no do's and don'ts in *dharma*, but only guidelines that an intelligent mind needs to understand and apply. It is situation and person dependent. If there were an edict – *Don't kill* Or *Avoid violence* – as an example, then how can it be *dharma?* True that killing is terrible, and violence – verbal or mental is bad, but is it bad on all occasions? What about the context? If we must follow such edicts, then we cannot even live. Because we cannot even eat anything. Eating, whether it is meat or plants necessarily involves violence. Killing animals is. Tilling the land is. And, if we chose to not eat at all, then aren't we demonstrating violence towards ourselves? How is that fair in the larger scheme of things? When we stretch it far enough, the illogicality of the edict comes across – we must stop breathing immediately. Even breath is killing unseen ecosystem of minute living beings.

Nuances of *Dharma* cannot be taught by logic. That's why our scriptures use the story-telling construct and explain its nuances. It is impossible for anyone to decode the *nuances,* and that's why we too, like Yudhishtira, need to take the guidance of Krishna. This is readily available to us even today in the form of *Bhagavad Gita.* And Mahabharata shares the application of *dharma* concept in so many beautiful stories that it is difficult not to develop a healthy perspective towards the principles behind those stories.

Using a beautiful metaphor of a tree, he compares Duryodhana to a mighty tree of anger. The tree was born of Duryodhana's selfish desire and had its roots in the blind attachment of the king Dhritarashtra. He also compares Yudhishtira like a great tree of *dharma,* with Krishna himself as its root, along with *Vedas* as well as learned, wise people supporting the tree.

Krishna's metaphor says it all.

Whatever is born out of blind attachment – selfish desire, anger, is not *dharma.*

Whatever that must be done to overcome selfish desire, anger, and even blind attachment is *dharma.*

I strongly believe that when we understanding the *dharmic* framework better, we are able to overcome our dilemmas by seeing the larger perspective before acting on our choices.

Gratitude

I owe my deep gratitude to Swami Tadatmananda whose excellent discourses on Mahabharata and his style to elucidate the principles of *dharma & karma* helped me shape my own thinking. I also want to express my deep respects to Swami Guruparananda, Swami Paramarthananda, and the entire *Arsha Vidya* Guru Parampara, without whose gentle guidance I would not even attempt this book. I am so very thankful to my parents, my wife, and children as well as to my fellow *Gita satsangis* and friends. Several friends, well-wishers and co-teachers at *Arsha Vidya Gurukulam* have shared their feedback and comments that helped me improve this offering I make to you.

I also acknowledge all those anonymous Reddit users, who provided the core ideas of human dilemmas that I attempted to write as stories. My humble offering of forty stories are meant to weave in and explain the philosophy of *dharma, karma* into common place life situations.

Hope you have fun reading these stories.

Shoes Off

Ravi woke up unusually early, the pre-dawn silence wrapping around him. In the quiet, he could hear gentle breaths of his sleeping children. Today was different – Sam was coming.

Anxiety pulsed in his veins, sharper than his usual morning routine. He shuffled out of bed to find Rani at the Puja corner, her prayers a gentle murmur. She smiled at him through half-closed eyes and stopped him from leaning in to kiss her forehead.

"No chappals here, Ravi. *Puja* corner, remember? It's a rule – and don't bring that American style here without a shower!" she teased lightly. Her voice was gentle, a reminder they were back in Bengaluru. In the Bay Area, neither Ravi nor the kids had heeded her daily pleas to leave their shoes outside. Now, back in India, she'd gotten her way.

He mumbled an apology and padded off to the bathroom. Memories of yesterday's preparations swirled in his head. Ravi especially wasn't a religious man, but he respected Rani's quirks, especially the no-*chappal* rule in the *puja* corner. Why God would mind footwear in their home, he couldn't fathom. The *puja* corner was just a part of their house, wasn't it?

As they prepared for the client visit, one last time yesterday, the company buzzed with nervous energy; mirroring Ravi's own. "Suits, jackets, polished shoes – the whole shebang!" he boomed at his team, the CEO voice echoing through the conference room. The management team, all in suits, nodded solemnly. Bonuses hung in the balance today. Sam's company was their biggest client, thirty percent of their revenue. Sam, the founder, was finally visiting after a decade of partnership.

"Let's go over the program again," Ravi continued. "We need to impress him with our tradition, our hospitality." This ritual was familiar, yet essential. All *desi* companies do it to impress their *gora* clients. Every new client got the royal treatment – a visit to remember. So far, it had worked wonders for Ravi too. Happy clients meant repeat business and growth. A formula that hadn't failed yet, from the lamp-lighting ceremony to the five-star dinner and, sometimes, a weekend getaway to BR Hills or Kabini. Rustic forest living for a few days, in an *ashram* like cottage, with no artificial lighting, lots of live jungle music from the birds, bees and trees to the constant *sruti*[3] of the flowing Kabini.

When the team gathered, Shobha, the sharp VP of sales and marketing, outlined the plan. "I'll pick Sam up and bring him straight here. At the door, you'll formally welcome him, Ravi. We have the six-foot brass lamp set up. You can invite him to light it. Bala and his team have done a fantastic job with the *rangoli*[4] and flowers. As he walks over, Sumitra will garland him and offer him a lighter."

---

3 Background hum

4 Traditionally, a pattern drawn on the ground usually using flour made from different colors.

Ravi interrupted, a flicker of doubt crossing his face. "Maybe I light the first wick, then Sam can follow? He might not know our customs…"

"Good idea," Shobha agreed, and continued, "After the lamp, demos and meetings. You know the drill for those, I presume?"

The big day arrived. The white Tesla glided into the campus. As the back door opened, the assembled team of twenty – from receptionists to executives – felt a wave of nervous anticipation. Shobha and Sam emerged.

People silently prayed to their favorite God, each asking for a smooth day and for nothing to go wrong. The techie prayed for a smooth demo, the VPs for the perfect pitch, Ravi for an impression that mirrored his leadership style, and the new office boy prayed against spilling coffee on his starched uniform.

Ravi shook Sam's hand, pleasantries exchanged, then ushered him towards the lamp ceremony. A majestic five-foot *kutthuvilakku*[5] dominated the reception, a vibrant *rangoli* adding a splash of color. A large screen displayed a welcome message, and Illayaraja's classical songs filled the air.

"May we begin with a traditional Indian custom?" Ravi gestured towards the lamp. Sam, looking genuinely impressed, nodded.

One of the VPs offered a matchbox. Ravi struck a match and lit one wick. A collective clap echoed as the lamp flickered to life. Ravi then passed the box to Sam.

---

5   A traditional lamp, usually made of alloy or metal, that uses oil and wick mechanism.

But Sam surprised them all. Instead of lighting the next wick, he stepped back, removed his shoes and socks, then lit the lamp while murmuring a short *Sanskrit* prayer[6] in a soft American accent, a touch of reverence despite the foreign tongue. Totally unexpected for a foreigner! Then, briefly folding his hands in a respectful *namaste*[7] to the lamp just lit, he moved backwards and slipped into his shoes as the applause roared even louder. In that instant, Ravi was reminded of Rani chiding him in the morning. A contrast of two people from different parts of the world. A chasm between modernity and traditions.

After the evening's dinner and drinks, Ravi dropped Sam off at his hotel, a strange hollowness settling in his gut. The day had gone well, but something felt off. How did Sam know the *desi* prayer? And why, oh why, did he have to take off his shoes in front of everyone? How did we miss understanding Sam?

Shobha's name flashed on his phone. He answered.

"Sam is a history student. He specializes in Eastern culture. And he knows India far more than we thought. He is a Sanskrit scholar. Sorry, we missed. Hope it won't affect our relationship with him." She spoke.

---

6   शुभं करोति कल्याणमारोग्यं धनसंपदा ।
शत्रुबुद्धिविनाशाय दीपज्योतिर्नमोऽस्तुते ॥
[Meaning: I pray to the light of the lamp that which brings auspiciousness, health wealth, and prosperity as well as destroys enemies in our mind – desire, anger, greed, attachment, ego, jealousy.]

7   Namaste is traditional Indian greeting, literally meaning, I recognize the same divinity within both of us.

Reaching home, he was greeted by Rani. "How was the meeting?" she inquired.

Ravi hung his head. "Maybe," he mumbled, "I should have practiced removing my *chappals* at home, near the *puja* corner."

Can't Marry an Orthodox

"I am sorry, I cannot marry you, Badri." Meg said.

Badri was speechless. They had just sat down for dinner at their favorite *desi* restaurant. *The date was not starting off right*, he thought.

"Why Meghana?"

"I can't accept having an orthodox partner," she added, "that's not how I imagined my life to be."

"Can you explain why you call me orthodox?" asked a surprised Badrinarayanan. He prided himself as traditional, not orthodox, or fundamentalist. And knew the difference between these words well.

"Mom told me that you wake up at 4AM daily and do sun-worship. I can't do that. I like to sleep in late." She was not so curious about customs and traditions. Her dad had neither practiced any such thing daily nor had explained to her ever.

"You mean *sandhyavandanam?*" he said.

"Yes. That sounds right. If we go to parties and are late, then we can't get up early. Or if you insist to still wake up at 4 every day, then we must curtail our social life. Either way, it is a lose-lose situation" she said.

Badri felt a wave of disappointment wash over him. He had really liked Meghana and envisioned a future together – he could see it clearly, a life with her, maybe even two kids. It had all seemed so perfectly aligned, even blessed by the panditji who confirmed that their horoscopes matched.

"Can't we work something out?" he asked quietly, hoping to hear a hint of openness in her voice.

But Meg shook her head. She slowly took off the engagement ring, laying it gently on the table. It wasn't easy to end things this way, she knew. Yet, she'd made up her mind. The ring lay between them, silent, as if waiting to see whether it would go back on her finger or disappear into his pocket forever.

He had suspected something and wanted to confirm.

"Do you know what *sandhyavandanam* is?" he asked.

"Sort of. I looked it up. On Wikipedia. It is some sort of a ritual that one must do daily three times." She said very casually, as if Wikipedia was the single source of truth for everything in this universe. Least of all matters that pertain to Hinduism and its practices.

Crowdsourcing is good for several topics, but not for this. But she did not know that.

"Do you know why we should do it?"

"Of course not. I browsed through the article and got the gist of it. It is impractical, seems archaic and I don't see any benefits."

He was silent. Processing what she said.

"I can explain the benefits of this practice. It is ancient and has been proven to be very beneficial not only for those who practice, but to **all** associated with the practitioner." he said, emphasizing the word *all*.

She did not ask him to explain. She did not want to. She had made up her mind to not take back the ring. She knew in that instant that this guy was not the guy she wanted to spend her life with. She liked it first when he called her Meghana, and not as Meg. But in the past month that they were engaged, he refused to address her as Meg and insisted on calling her full name. Not just that, she was also annoyed that he preferred to be addressed by his full name. A long one – although not a tongue twister.

All these were proof that he belonged to the orthodox category.

Her parents persuaded her to try the arranged marriage route. She was already going on her early thirties and the constant refrain from her mom – *your biological time clock is ticking* was beyond irritating. Perhaps that is what her mom wanted in the first place. For her to act.

He remained silent, not volunteering any more information about his daily ritual. The silence stretched awkwardly, pressing her to speak. It was the bone of contention and the ring lying in between them must choose one of them now.

"Once we are married, initially you will not insist; but I fear that you may ask me to wake up at 4AM too to do the sun-worship. I cannot do that. I am a night owl." she slowly said.

That's when he raised his head and looked into her eyes. He looked relieved.

Did I say something wrong? Meg thought.

He smiled gently, picked up the ring, and said, "I am glad that we figured out that our marriage will not work."

At that instant, Badrinarayanan knew certainly, that she was a coconut – brown from outside and all white inside. Although he never used that derogatory word before even in friendly conversations, it was apt to describe the cultural transition Meghana had made.

As he walked away from the table towards the door, with the ring in his pocket, he told Meghana, "Being traditional doesn't mean being orthodox or rigid. I like to follow a helpful tradition. Helpful not just for me but for all. FYI, traditionally women don't have to do *sandhyavandanam*. It is a practice ordained only for some men, and when they do it, the benefits accrue to **all** in the house. And, I am glad we found out this bone of contention before we are married."

And, just like that Badrinarayanan walked towards his car.

Meghana was relieved that Badri was not upset with the decision, but she became extremely curious. As soon as she sat in her car, she googled the meanings of the words to realize that being traditional does not mean one is rigid like an orthodox or a fundamentalist. Suddenly, she felt so let down by her sources of wisdom – the Internet, on this topic.

Benefits to all – how could that be and only men – Why?

As she pondered this, a thought lingered – *I should just have called Mani mama in Chennai to learn more. Or better, mami would have told her if she were waking up at 4AM to do Sandhyavandanam.*

She called *mama & mami* the very instant the thought crossed her mind.

Grand Happening

Ravi, a first-generation Indian immigrant in California, beamed with pride as he surveyed his backyard. His first attempt at a vegetable garden, tended with long evenings of watering and frantic internet searches for pest control, had yielded a bounty beyond his wildest dreams. Squash, plump and orange, practically overflowed the raised vegetable beds.

His family, used to more modest vegetable hauls in India, looked at the harvest with wide eyes. Even after generous distributions to friends and relatives, mountains of squash still threatened to take over the yard. It was time to share the surplus. With a flourish, Ravi decided to spread his bounty to the neighborhood.

He carefully selected the ripest squash, filling a large wicker basket. On a sheet of paper, he scrawled a bold "FREE" and taped it to the basket's handle. With a satisfied smile, he placed it on his porch, just beside the open front door.

Settling back on the couch, he sipped a cup of *chai,* his eyes occasionally darting toward the porch. Soon, a young couple from across the street tentatively approached the basket. After a quick glance around, they each picked a squash and hurried back to their house. A wave of neighborly warmth washed over Ravi. This was exactly what he'd hoped for—a small act of kindness, a shared harvest that brought people together.

An hour later, he was still glued to the couch, watching neighbors' gesture at his door or murmur thanks as they took a squash. He basked in the quiet glory of being the green-thumbed neighbor who cared for his community.

Suddenly, his smile faltered. A sleek silver car pulled up in front of his house, and two tall, impeccably dressed women stepped out. Ravi watched, a frown creasing his forehead, as they strode purposefully toward the porch. He braced himself to greet them, perhaps offer a few friendly squash recipes. But instead, they simply scooped up the entire basket and tossed it nonchalantly into the back of their car—without a word of thanks, not even a passing glance his way.

Ravi fumed. **"These people,"** he muttered, **"no manners, no respect for others' hard work."** Disappointment gnawed at him. He'd imagined a steady trickle of neighbors, each taking a squash and complimenting his green thumb. The women's brash act had shattered that image. It wasn't just about the squash anymore; it was about his pride, his need for acknowledgment.

The next morning, a pang of guilt woke Ravi early. He decided to take a walk to clear his head. As he strolled through the bustling Saturday flea market, a familiar figure caught his eye. It was one of the women from yesterday, standing behind a stall. She looked different—her hair pulled back in a messy bun; her designer clothes replaced by a simple apron. Steam rose from a large cauldron behind her, and a line of people, mostly men and women with careworn faces, stretched out in front of her stall.

Hesitantly, Ravi approached to see what she was serving. A ladleful of steaming orange soup landed in a paper cup, accompanied by a thick slice of crusty bread. She was feeding the homeless. The rich aroma of roasted vegetables and spices filled the air.

His gaze fell on a small, hand-painted sign propped beside the cauldron. It read: **"Free Squash Soup! Thank that unknown neighbor!"**

Shame washed over Ravi. He hadn't considered the countless hours the woman had spent turning his surplus into a nourishing meal for those in need.

"I was needy, too," he thought, though in a different way. In his desire for recognition, he'd overlooked the bigger picture. The sunshine, the rain, the fertile earth, even the birds, bees, and earthworms had all played a role in his bountiful harvest. It wasn't just his work alone.

The realization struck him like a bolt of lightning. His pride so easily inflated—not only by the bounty of his garden but also the newly purchased home he'd acquired after selling his company—needed a sharp prick.

Perhaps, he thought, there truly was a grand happening in this universe, one that he was simply a part of. His role, like everyone else's, was to do his bit.

He remembered a verse from the Bhagavad Gita, a scripture his grandfather had often quoted, which he'd once argued against: "***Nimitta matram bhava***"—**Be just an instrument in my hands**. In a flash, the wisdom of the verse seeped into his mind. Ravi bowed his head, a newfound humility settling in.

The woman hadn't simply taken his squash. She'd fulfilled a purpose—her role in a grander scheme of things.

Bella Bevu

A arti hit send on her group chat message, a surge of excitement in her chest. It was the official onset of spring, after all. **"Happy *Ugadi*, everyone! Here's to a prosperous new year filled with fresh beginnings!"**

The *panchanga*—a piece of art in numbers—captured the intricate "movement" of the sun, moon, earth, constellations, and other celestial bodies influencing life on earth. It was astronomy on paper, a form of science expressing relative motion, with complex calculations of celestial movements distilled into a simple, useful guide for everyday life. When the moon moved into the *Chitra* constellation, it marked the new year with the onset of spring and the end of winter. Aarti knew that Ugadi was the Anglicized form of *Yugadi*, a compound of *yug* (age) and *adi* (beginning). In North India, the festival was celebrated as *Gudi Padwa* or *Cheti Chand*. The striking similarity between *Chitra* and *Cheti* didn't escape her, nor did the significance of *Chand* (moon), symbolizing the moon's movement across the heavens.

It was, indeed, a big deal—a reason *desis* celebrated it with grand festivity.

Ugadi, marked by beautiful *rangolis* and delectable *mango pachadi*, held a special place in her heart. But after four years in the U.S., something felt amiss. Despite living in the

Bay Area—where finding a *desi* was as easy as throwing a stone—she still couldn't find *neem* flowers. In her hometown of Davanagare, eating bitter *neem* flowers mixed with sweet *jaggery* on Ugadi was a cherished tradition, a reminder of life's bitter-sweet nature and a gentle, annual reinforcement to accept both with grace.

Yet her group chat, a sprawling digital hub of over 200 colleagues, remained silent. Aarti scrolled through her phone, checking for missed notifications, but there was nothing. A frown creased her brow. Her friends were mostly work colleagues, and now she felt a twinge of neglect. Her Ugadi message seemed to have vanished into the digital void.

The next day, however, the group chat buzzed with a different kind of energy. *Eid* greetings filled the feed—a vibrant tapestry of messages and well wishes. Aarti scrolled through, feeling a strange mix of emotions. Hindu friends who'd barely acknowledged her Ugadi message were now enthusiastically participating in *Eid* celebrations.

"Happy *Eid*, everyone!" chimed in her teammate and a close friend who hadn't responded to her Ugadi greeting. **"May this festival bring you joy and blessings!"**

Aarti sighed.

It wasn't the act of wishing a happy *Eid* that bothered her. She, too, had sent warm wishes to her friends, genuinely sharing in their joy.

But the stark contrast was hard to ignore. In a company that prided itself on diversity and inclusion, why was *Ugadi*— celebrated by so many in the company—treated as less worthy of acknowledgment? Could it be that her friends and colleagues, coming from all corners of the world, knew more about *Eid* but nothing about *Ugadi*? Was it that people weren't truly inclusive? Or was she just reading too much into it?

And what about her Hindu friends? Did they not understand the cultural significance of Ugadi, the hopes and prayers for a bright new year? Or did they want to distance themselves deliberately from Indian culture and traditions? If so, why?

Her logical mind failed her, leaving her with no answers. And her emotional mind felt the weight of disappointment. Aarti shut her phone with a soft click. It wasn't about getting hundreds of likes; it was about a simple acknowledgment and a shared celebration of one's own culture.

She sighed, recognizing a kind of "wokeism" in her colleagues, even a dangerous form of colonized thinking among some of her fellow Hindus at work.

Then she smiled, reminding herself that life is, indeed, sweet-bitter—*bella-bevu*[8].

---

8   *Bella* – jaggery and *bevu* – neem flower

Bigoted Boss

Ramana switched on his laptop, the familiar hum of the morning video call filling his ears. He had woken up an hour early, completed his morning routine, and prepared for this important call ahead of the big release.

Adjusting his camera to avoid the morning light washing him out, he caught a glance of his reflection on the screen. A strong horizontal line of *vibhuti*, the sacred ash, marked his forehead between his brows—a part of his morning ritual that centered him before the day began.

As the call started, Krish, his peer who had set up the meeting, asked Ramana to explain the deliverables and what they would mean for users. Ramana was about to begin, flipping to the agenda slide, when his senior colleague and team lead, Radha, burst onto the screen, coffee cup in hand and voice laced with forced cheer. She was three minutes late.

Interrupting, she called out, "Good morning, everyone! Especially Ramana, with the, uh, interesting mark on his forehead today."

Ramana felt a flicker of irritation, though he had learned patience over the years of working with Radha. "Good morning, Radha," he greeted with a smile. "This is *vibhuti*. I wear it every day."

"*Vibhuti*?" Radha's voice took on a playful lilt. "Is that some kind of new coffee filter? Does it give you a morning energy boost?"

Normally, Ramana might have chuckled at her teasing. But not today. "Not quite. It's a religious mark."

"Religious?" Radha's smile vanished, replaced by a frown. In a mocking tone, she added, "Then I should be asking you for *aashirwad*[9], *Panditji*."

Sensing the tension, Krish tried to smooth things over. "Perhaps we can move on to the agenda, Radha? We can discuss Ramana's, uh, interesting coffee filter later." Krish, though sensitive, was hesitant to stand up to Radha—especially after she had lashed out at him earlier in the month over a minor delay.

Radha was a paradox. A second-generation Indian American, she was a fast tracker in the corporate world. Her family had immigrated to the U.S. when her parents were young, leaving behind the traditions and rituals of their homeland. Her parents had given her a *desi* name, likely influenced by her grandparents, but they had embraced an American way of life. Diwali was just an excuse for fancy lights and food at her aunt's house, and Holi meant powder fights at college parties. Religion, for Radha, was a distant cultural footnote with no real significance.

But Radha wasn't done talking.

She pressed on, "No, Krish, I think this is important. We need to maintain a professional environment. Work and religion should be separate."

____

9   blessings

Ramana sighed inwardly. Here we go again, he thought. Today, however, he felt compelled to address it directly. Radha was always obnoxious, but this was getting under his skin.

"Radha," he began, calm yet firm, "I missed part of my routine to join this call, and I don't think I deserve this."

Radha, probably catching the unspoken words in his tone, seemed riled by his retort. She countered, "I don't think this attire of yours would be suitable in business meetings. Especially with clients."

That was the last straw. Ramana had always been humble, a quality he held dear. He was a smart IIT graduate, a ten-pointer who had worked at multiple Bay Area startups. With his background and skills, offers were never far from his inbox. At that moment, he decided he could no longer tolerate Radha's intolerance.

"Two things," he said calmly.

"One, this mark is made from holy ash, and I wear it daily. It reminds me to stay humble, reminding me that all achievements and wealth are fleeting— ashes, in the end. It's a valuable way to keep our egos in check."

The choice of words seemed to sting Radha, but she still pushed back. "But it's distracting, Ramana. We wasted time on this instead of business. How can we avoid this?"

"It was you who was late for the meeting," Ramana replied, his irritation surfacing. "And secondly, this is a 6 a.m. call. We're on Zoom, and I'm in my home. This meeting is already infringing on my space, and on my morning *puja* routine."

The call went silent. The other attendees, wary of Radha's influence, remained passive, their faces frozen in awkward silence on screen.

Then, breaking the tension, Ramana spoke two words: "I quit."

With that, he shut his laptop and returned to his morning *puja*.

Saptapadi Saat Samundar Paar[10]

Sriram and Rekha's kitchen filled with the comforting aroma *shahi paneer* in their American home, now filled with an uncomfortable silence. Their son, Ravi, wouldn't be joining them for the first time in years; he was "shacking up" with his girlfriend, Mei, as he'd phrased it so nonchalantly.

Sriram crumbled his *roti* in silence, feeling a mix of emotions. They'd raised Ravi in Chicago, hoping he'd be a blend of American openness and Indian tradition. They wanted him to have his freedom, to explore, to choose his own path. But this? This felt like a betrayal of everything they held sacred. *A live-in relationship*, Rekha thought, dabbing her eyes. "He's just twenty-two, Sriram," she murmured, her voice weighed down by her own upbringing that revered marriage as life's foundation.

Rekha had grown up in a traditional South Indian family, taught that marriage was more than a relationship. It was a path to inner growth, an opportunity for two individuals to become selfless, to mature together. "It's not about arranged or love marriage," she whispered. "It's about *commitment*."

Sriram, a logical man in most things, felt a strange twist of regret and even guilt. He wondered if their hands-off

______

10   'Seven Steps in the lands beyond seven seas': a play on words related to a marriage ritual and distant lands.

parenting, their desire to be "cool" parents, had somehow backfired. Should they have taught him more about their cultural beliefs? About the meaning of marriage beyond the vows and rings? "Maybe he should have gone to Chinmaya Mission classes as a kid," he murmured aloud, thinking of other families who balanced Indian values with modern life.

Memories flickered through Sriram's mind: their wedding, the chants, the mantras, the solemn promises of the *Saptapadi*, the seven steps around the sacred fire, each step a vow to walk together as friends, as partners, as a unit. Those vows were meant to be the foundation of a life. For Ravi, raised on Hollywood rom-coms and casual relationships, it likely all felt outdated, just a bunch of rigid rituals.

Rekha broke the silence with a tear gliding down her cheek. "*Compatibility is important.* I'm not saying we need horoscopes matched anymore. But commitment isn't just about living together and sharing a pizza, Sriram. It's about standing by each other, through thick and thin, through changes. And if he's committed, why won't he marry her? That would give me peace of mind." Her voice grew thick with worry. "People change, Sriram. Feelings change. Mei might not see the world the same way in a few years, and neither might Ravi. They'll face hardships, they'll hurt each other—who will keep them from walking away?"

Her voice softened. "*Marriage,* with all its customs, teaches us selflessness. I still remember our own wedding vows, each of those seven steps. The first step itself—'may we walk together for nourishment, and with mutual respect and protection.' That's just the beginning of what it means to be committed, Sriram. The rest… it means building a life together, brick by sacred brick."

Sriram listened, seeing a new side of his wife that he'd taken for granted in their years together. He'd known her as a steady partner, but he'd never considered just how deeply she believed in their shared values, even if she hadn't always known them consciously. "What exactly is bothering you, Rekha?" he asked, a bit impatient but drawn to understand her more deeply.

She took a steadying breath. "I feel like we've failed, Sriram. We didn't teach Ravi about life beyond the basics—study, work, save. We didn't teach him that fulfillment comes from something beyond this cycle of earning and spending. Maybe he and Mei would see the value in our customs, in their purpose, if only we'd shown him."

Sriram took her words in, feeling their truth settle heavily on his heart. He remembered the early days of their marriage, when each step around the fire was shrouded in mystery for him too. Their love hadn't started immediately, but it had deepened with each year. The *Saptapadi* had seemed a formal tradition back then, but now, with time, he recognized the wisdom in those seven vows: a promise to nourish each other, to grow together, to protect one another, to share in health, wealth, harmony, and peace.

"How could he understand all that?" Rekha continued. "He's surrounded by a world that treats commitment like a trial run, cancelable if things get uncomfortable. But marriage is a bond that grows richer over time, even through hardship.

It helps us learn humility, to live with another person even when things aren't perfect."

Rekha's eyes glistened with hope. "It's not too late, Sriram. I've been reading more lately, and teaching the young ones at Chinmaya Mission has taught me so much about our own culture. If Ravi could see it that way, maybe he'd understand. Maybe Mei would too."

Sriram listened, unsure but willing to try. That evening, he watched as Rekha dug out an old wedding album. She flipped through the photos, touching the images of their younger selves. "Remember our *Saptapadi*, Sriram?" she murmured, her voice soft. "We were nervous and excited, and maybe a little scared. But we took those steps together, a promise for a lifetime."

He nodded, feeling the memories surface. "Maybe we should show them," he said after a pause. "Not just tell, but show them what we believe."

The next day, they called Ravi, tentative but hopeful. To their surprise, he agreed to a visit. As they packed, they made sure to bring their wedding album and a video, hopeful that this bridge, these symbols of their lives together, would help explain. They had found themselves here, seven seas away, but the wisdom of their traditions still held. In that moment, they knew that in seeking to reach Ravi and Mei, they were taking the first step of a new *Saptapadi*, walking together in understanding, *saat samundar paar*, across the seven seas.

Janus Face

Neelam stared at the blinking cursor on her LinkedIn post, a knot of tension tightening in her stomach. Three days had passed since the Supreme Court's decision, and the anger simmered beneath the surface. Finally, she typed, her fingers flying across the keyboard. "My body, my choice. I can't but disagree with the decision. Anyone who wants a place to stay to get an abortion done and recover, DM me."

As a Senior VP in a tech company, Neelam wielded influence. Her voice, amplified by thousands of followers across social media, had the power to spark a movement. But putting her stance out there left her feeling vulnerable and exposed. She carried secrets that no one else knew.

The next morning, as she entered the office, she spotted Jane, a staunch conservative colleague, across the hallway. A premonition of a tense day washed over Neelam. Jane offered a curt nod, her disapproval hanging heavy in the air. Thankfully, Vinita, a colleague with similar views to her, broke the tension with a warm smile and a supportive, "Loved your post today, Neelam." Likes and messages of solidarity trickled in, a wave of encouragement. But life had a way of moving on. Soon, Neelam was caught in the familiar vortex of work deadlines. And the hoopla on social media died off. Everyone said what they had to say and after a week, their inner sense reminded them that there are bills to pay, promotions to be sought and the show called life must go on.

She dreaded the weekly phone calls with her mother back in India. Her mom's single-track agenda always monopolized their thirty-minute conversations, which still appeared in her calendar as 'call parents' – an entry she couldn't bring herself to change after her father's death. Her dad had struggled in the last few weeks. She was there with him. All the time. Not only was she a darling to him, but she also loved him too. She was his rock. She could not bear to see the tubes in every hole from his body.

And she had asked her mom many times. *Mama, should we pull the plug and let papa go?* But her mom said a firm *no* every time she asked. *Nahi kar sakte hai. Paap hai. Jitna din woh rahenge, utna din main unki dekhbhal karoongi.(We can't do that. It's a sin. I will care for him as long as he lives.)*

After her dad passed away, she became the top priority for her mom.

"Shaadi kar le. You're already past your prime!" her refrain went, a constant reminder of the societal pressure to settle down. This time, however, Neelam surprisingly agreed to a blind date set up by her mother – Nirav, a seemingly compatible match based on their horoscopes.

Their first date flowed easily. Both delved into shared interests – movies, food, work, travel – finding common ground. A spark seemed to have been ignited between them, and Neelam found herself looking forward to their frequent outings.

One evening, the conversation took an unexpected turn.

"Look at that adorable toddler," Nirav remarked, pointing to a nearby table. "I love kids. I want at least three, someday."

Neelam braced herself, shifting uncomfortably in her chair as she felt a cold sweat forming.

Nirav continued, his voice laced with a subtle disappointment, "Children are a gift. Yet, there are so many couples struggling to conceive, while others…" he trailed off.

Neelam understood his unspoken implication – the current abortion debate. "Women should have control over their bodies," she stated firmly.

"Pro-choice, are you?" Nirav inquired.

He pulled out his phone, quickly finding the statistics[11]. 'In 2023, there were one million abortions in the US,' he said, 'while two million couples waited to adopt.'"

They discussed the Supreme Court decision, and from her perspective the regressive shift in the US, and for all its shortcomings of being a developing country – India's recent legalization of abortion.

A clash of perspectives emerged. "Laws may change," Nirav argued, "but morals transcend them. It's a personal choice rooted in ethics."

---

11   https://www.cnn.com/2024/03/18/health/abortion-data-guttmacher/index.html and https://www.americanadoptions.com/pregnant/waiting_adoptive_families#:~:text=While%20it%20is%20difficult%20to,who%20is%20placed%20for%20adoption.

Neelam countered, "Morality is subjective. Laws provide a framework for a functioning society."

"What do you think of prostitution then?" His question was not belligerent but inquisitive. And in the context of Neelam being pro-choice, it was pertinent he thought.

"I am pro-choice when it comes to abortion. Prostitution is illegal in US, both of us know." She spoke, a bit angrily.

"So is abortion now after Roe v Wade was overturned. Either we choose to respect laws or decide to analyze this threadbare based on first principles. If pro-life argument is *my body, my choice,* then don't they have choice to do what they can with their body any time?" Nirav asked. It was getting somehow important for him to know. He liked her too and was imagining a life with her. He held the view that nothing was black and white, including abortion and was situation dependent. He knew – *exceptional circumstances like rape, incest or danger to the mother's life could be reasons for abortion. He was not sure. However, he was sure of this – there is no valid moral argument for terminating a pregnancy caused due to carelessness or willful abandon. Both parties are equally responsible, and they must let nature run its course. Like a car accident. We cannot undo once it has happened.*

His question was logical and direct. Neelam had researched the science. The fetus (*she liked to not call it a baby in womb*) was a separate DNA from the host (*and she did not like to use the term, mother either*). No technicality in that at all. *Nirav is indeed asking me a logical question. A prostitute is living up to 'my body, my choice' position truly.* She had to acknowledge. But did not show it to Nirav.

She squirmed at the question. Looked away from his gentle yet sharp eyes. She did not have a position on what was right or wrong. She had thought of various circumstances a woman gets pregnant.

"And what do you think of euthanasia?" He really wanted to know. Her silence had burst the first bubble of his imaginary future with her.

Fortunately for Neelam, the server brought dessert, and their conversation reached an impasse. But Neelam's mind drifted back to a time capsule locked away in her past – Ned, her first love from Berkeley, and the life-altering decision that forever changed their world.

A missed period, a doctor's confirmation, and a swirl of emotions followed – fear, uncertainty, and dreams suddenly threatened by the life growing inside her. The doctor had showed her the baby in her womb. A tiny creature., just a mere outline of a human, growing within her womb. Starting off as a single-celled zygote, the cells rapidly and continuously had grown in the three months. The gynecologist showed her the neural tube which will become the brain and spine. She saw two pairs of ten tiny buds – the genesis of fingers and toes. Three distinct parts were visible in the creature within her womb, all less than one sixth of an inch – which the doc explained as future head, trunk, and legs.

Faced with an unplanned pregnancy, the decision for an abortion was agonizing but ultimately clear. Ned, however, reacted with outrage. He saw it as a betrayal, the snuffing out of a potential life.

"We are just twenty-two. And I have a future planned."

"But the baby happened. I am equally responsible. Yet you decided without even letting me know." He said, eyes blood-shot.

"It's your ego speaking. I think you also don't want to be burdened by this unplanned pregnancy." She said, well-knowing Ned's background and respect for all life. She had teased him several times about his vegetarianism and won the argument that plants had life too and by eating them, he was killing life.

Ned had left her the very day after a bitter argument leaving a gaping wound in Neelam's heart. She loved him and knew would be happy with him. But, the thing became a wedge between them.

Nirav's sudden mention of a "cosmic law" sparked a fresh wave of guilt, a burden she'd carried for a decade. She did not hear what he had said, but those two words reverberating in her ears. The memory of her mother's impassioned plea against abortion echoed in her mind.

The last conversation on the topic with her mother now seemed to add fuel to the fire. A few months ago, before she aborted Ned's baby, the wise mom had sensed her live-in relationship and had directly told her.

*""Baccha kabhi mat giraana" (Never terminate a pregnancy), her mother had said. "The Panditji says *Bhrūṇahatyā* is one of the worst sins. There is no repentance for this crime."*

And, Neelam, if ever you are in that situation, irrespective of the circumstances you are in or any birth defects with the baby, promise me you will deliver the baby." And she had added, "We must let nature run its course. That is why I never agreed to your suggestion about pulling the plug for your dad. It would have been a murder that I would not have been able to live with myself afterwards.

She had hesitated then to promise. And, her mom added, "I will raise the child for you, till you settle down. My arthritis issue aside, I will come to US and take care of the baby. Just promise me."

She had humored her and promised. A false one. And, even now, her mom knew nothing about it.

Tears welled up as she excused herself from dinner, leaving the tiramisu untouched. Never to meet Nirav again. Back in her apartment, she cried when Netflix conspired and recommended "Reversing Roe." She flipped the channel. Roku was recommending *Mimi,* a Bollywood movie about a small town struggling actress who becomes a surrogate mother for a white couple, but her experience takes unexpected turns. Overwhelmed, she switched off the TV, seeking solace in a bottle of Smirnoff.

The vodka, as it flowed down her throat, only fueled the embers of long-dormant emotions. Flames of unexplained loss erupted, consuming her with guilt, shame, and fear. Love and trust, both violated, burned within her. It always ended this way, yet she continued carrying the weight, not knowing a better way than the far from helpful vodka method.

It was getting heavier as time went by. *It would have been just nine months and a few pounds more then. But this weight is growing. Unbearably.*

How many more years must I hide my Janus face?

She cried into the night; the silent walls witness to her familiar, broken lament.

Meat Conflict

The aroma of simmering sambar filled the air, a familiar comfort in Anita's meticulously clean California kitchen. Just the new pots & pans and silverware she bought a week ago was giving a fresh look to her kitchen.

Her daughter, Anya, a cherubic bundle of nine years, sat at the table, meticulously separating the tofu from her vegetables. "Ugh, Mom, can't we have something besides *sambhar* & rice?" she grumbled.

The Sunday lunch of tofu & veggies with rice was a disaster and her plans to make nice *sambhar* for the evening did not seem to go well with Anya.

Anita sighed; her smile strained. "What would you like to eat?"

Anya was a picky eater. She did not want many vegetables. Neither she liked *dal.* And, Anita had to figure out how to make exotic dishes with cauliflower, potato, and peas being her favorites. And *paneer.* When the girl was five, and on those days when Anita ran out of *paneer* in the fridge, she had made "*mutter-paneer* without *paneer*"! And had told Anya that it was a name of a new dish! Anya enjoyed eating that, little realizing that mom was cheating her. But the trick stopped working soon.

Anya rolled her eyes and looked down at the floor. "Everyone else at school eats hamburgers and stuff. Why can't we?"

The question hung heavy in the air. She responded as she always did. "We will think about it." Anita, a first-generation Indian American, had tried her best to raise Anya a vegetarian, like she was brought up by her parents. But America, the land of melting pots and sizzling grills, and the crazy power of social media was proving to be a powerful influence on immigrant *desi* adults too, what to talk of young Anya.

Later that week, Santosh and Lakshmi, Anita's parents, arrived from India for a long-awaited visit. The reunion was a whirlwind of hugs, excited chatter, and the presentation of gifts – a silk sari for Anita, a miniature model of the famous black and yellow auto for Anya.

Anita's work pressure had mounted in the recent weeks, and she had made a frantic call to her parents to come over and support her. Hitting the road before the traffic to drive to SF and getting back late in the evening, was draining her. Her daily routine was not an envy to anyone. She prepared breakfast and lunch *dabba* for Anya before her drive., while grabbing a toast and coffee enroute in the car. Eight in the evening was the earliest she saw Anya in the day. Except for the weekends, when they spent time together. The past few weeks she had to work many weekends too, thanks to a major release they were doing. And she was a senior VP of the engineering and set standards to her team by showing up at work.

And the bitter separation from Jai had only complicated matters for her. Her parents were already upset about the divorce. She kept the reason for divorce a secret from her parents.

With her parents around, she breathed easily. Anya will have someone to receive her when she comes home after school.

And, when she gets back home, *Amma* would have cooked dinner for her too.

After spending the first weekend with her family, taking them grocery shopping to replenish the empty shelves for the next week, and customary temple visits, she knew she had to get back on the grind for weeks at stretch.

Anya walked in home from school. She got a warm welcome and hugs from her grandparents. *Ammamma* had made her favorite, aloo *gobi*. Anya beamed looking at the dining table.

Then all hell broke loose. She pulled out something from the school bag. It was a half-eaten big Mac.

Santosh's smile faltered. What type of burger? In his granddaughter's mouth? The thought sent a shiver down his spine. He exchanged a worried glance with Lakshmi. This wasn't what they expected. He didn't say a word to Anya.

Did Anita knew?

Later that night, after Anya was tucked in, Santosh and Lakshmi sat stiffly in the living room, a heavy silence hanging between them. As soon as Anita walked in, her dad shot the first salvo.

"Did you know?" Santosh finally asked, his voice laced with disappointment.

A surprised Anita looked quizzed. She shook her head, tears welling up in her eyes. "No, *Nanna*. I had no idea. I always pack her a vegetarian lunchbox, and she never complained."

"Maybe you need to talk to her and learn what she is eating at school. She is young and we can get her change her habits" Lakshmi offered, a sliver of hope in her voice.

"But wouldn't she have told you?" Santosh countered.

Anita bit her lip.

"I never asked." She spoke.

After the divorce, she was struggling as a single parent. Work was consuming her. Not only had she had missed picking up Anya at school many times, but she just did also not know what the girl did the entire day. Not even sure if she locked the front door!

She knew her parents. They were very traditional; farmers from Narasaraopet. Her father became a vegetarian by choice and their ancestors adopted Gandhian values. She grew up imbibing the food practices and culture they followed. She knew what to eat and what not to. She was not as strict as her parents who would not dine in any restaurant that served veg and non-veg.

The next morning, the usually cheerful breakfast table was subdued. Anita stole nervous glances at Anya, who seemed oblivious of what happened in the evening as she munched on her toast. Finally, she blurted out, "Anya, honey, what did you bring back from school yesterday?"

Anya looked up, a mischievous glint in her eyes. "A Big Mac, Mom! It was the best one ever!"

The air crackled with tension. Santosh put down his *chai* with a sigh. "Anya, do you know what a Big Mac is made of?"

Anya's smile faltered. "Uh, meat?" she mumbled, avoiding his gaze.

Lakshmi gasped, her hand flying to her mouth and Santosh walked away from the table. He could not hear anymore.

Anita said. "But Anya, how can you...?" Her voice trailed off, choked with emotion. The sacred cow, revered for generations, reduced to a fast-food patty. Anita felt a wave of guilt wash over her. *How would she know the difference between chicken and beef?Or veg and non-veg?*

"Anya," she said, her voice trembling, "we don't eat beef in our family. You know that don't you?"

Anya shrugged, her lower lip jutting out in defiance. "But everyone else at school eats it, Mom. It's just a burger."

"It's not 'just a burger,' Anya," Santosh said sternly. "The cow is a sacred animal in our culture. We revere it, we respect it." His voice trailed off, choked with emotion.

The conversation that followed was fraught with tears, frustration, and a deep sense of disconnect and broken sacred family values. Anya, a budding girl yearning to fit in with her peers, couldn't understand her grandparents' vehement reaction. And mom had never asked her what she ate at school. Santosh and Lakshmi, on the other hand, felt they did not belong here.

It was just a week since they had come from India. With plans to stay for six months and help Anita manage things and move on from the divorce.

Mealtime became strained, the joy of their parents' visit replaced by a constant undercurrent of tension in Anita's mind. Meanwhile her parents unable to reconcile themselves to Anya's dietary choices, found themselves increasingly withdrawn.

One evening, as Anita sat alone in the living room, Santosh approached her, his face etched with sadness. "Anita," he began, his voice low, "we've decided."

She looked at her dad. "We want to go back this weekend. I just rebooked our tickets."

Anita's eyes filled with tears. "*Nanna… Amma…* please…"

Lakshmi hugged her tightly, and Anita finally broke down. In a rush of emotion, she confessed what she had hidden from them.

"It was Jai," she said, her voice barely above a whisper. "He wanted to eat meat and encouraged Anya too. The fridge was filled with it. We fought about it every day. Eventually… it was one of the reasons for the divorce." She sniffed, wiping her eyes. "After he left, I threw away all the pots and pans. I bought new ones just before you came."

Lakshmi's embrace tightened as she whispered, "Oh, dear…." Santosh's face softened, his stern expression melting into understanding. They held their daughter, feeling the weight of the choices and challenges she faced alone.

The tension of the past few days slowly dissolved, replaced by quiet support as they silently promised to stay by her side.

Retirement Reflections

The rhythmic thump of the bass vibrated through the floor, and I felt my knees throb in protest. Here I was, celebrating my retirement amidst a crowd of young colleagues. They were all on the dance floor, faces flushed, voices loud with laughter and revelry, while I lingered near the edge, watching. A group of women swarmed around Sarah, the vibrant marketing head, who held court with her wine glass raised.

At sixty, I'd come to terms with my decision to leave. I had founded this company and led as COO, and now, watching the office's average age plummet as I left, it felt like the right time to step away. My life, after Chitra's death, had grown increasingly quiet. My children had their own lives, and though work had once filled a space that grief left behind, lately, even that spark had dimmed. Retirement was the next chapter, but what would it look like? I'd sold my house and planned to return to India. Perhaps I'd find answers there.

A voice suddenly cut through my thoughts. "Did you hear that?" one of the women squealed over the music. "Sarah got rid of Michael last week!" Her words sparked a wave of cheers, and Sarah, a statuesque redhead, held her glass high with a grin.

Then Sarah shouted joyfully, "It was the happiest day of my life!" A collective gasp rippled through the room, followed by a wave of boisterous cheers. She held aloft a glass of champagne, the ice clinking in a toast to her own liberation.

I watched it all unfold with a mix of amusement and a strange sense of yearning. Sarah and her husband, Michael, had been the picture-perfect couple. I had met them couple of times at office parties but did not know about the divorce. They were young, vibrant, and always seemed to be on the same wavelength – laughing at the same jokes, finishing each other's sentences. They were the ones who'd brought their adorable daughter, Lily, to company picnics, her face perpetually smeared with cake frosting.

But somewhere along the way, the laughter had died down. Sarah, a social butterfly, craved the thrill of crowded bars and exotic vacations. Michael, on the other hand, preferred quiet evenings curled up with a book. Their once-complementary differences had morphed into chasms they couldn't bridge. Lily, caught in the crossfire, became increasingly withdrawn, her smile turning fragile.

Reena, who had taken over my role, passed by with her own glass of wine. She leaned in. "Swami, I bet you never knew. The divorce was fast. Brutal. People took sides, and whispers went around. But looking at her tonight, I kind of get it."

"Which part?" I asked, genuinely curious.

She smirked, moving back to the dance floor with a wave, as if dismissing my question as naïve. Yet I lingered on it. Who decides happiness? What makes a person stay or leave, love or let go?

Walking back to my apartment, the thoughts stirred in my mind, and I replayed the evening in my head. In Sarah's exuberance, I saw a pattern taking shape. Happiness, I began to realize, wasn't a destination, nor was it bound to marriage or singledom. It was a choice made each day, a decision to dance with life as it changed, rather than waiting for a perfect moment. In Sarah's exuberance, I saw a narrative emerge.

Happiness, I realized, wasn't a destination, it wasn't a trophy earned at the altar or discarded in a courtroom. It was a journey, a constant dance with change and growth. In that room, I saw reflections of that same yearning for happiness in everyone. John, the quiet accountant, was talking animatedly to Leslie, a shy smile playing on his lips. He had a thing for her. I knew it. A secret desire for connection leading to better things and happiness. He sought happiness in that connection, and Sarah sought the same thing by breaking up the connection. Then I saw Swati. Swati, the geek was so busy explaining the thrill she got bungee jumping to the crowd. And Reena. She was reveling in the admiration of her colleagues.

Perhaps, the happiness we all crave isn't a singular, monumental event. It is not a place. Nor a thing. Neither a person. It is a decision to prioritize happiness in life. Then, events become just that, and we stop applying labels on them – happy or unhappy (event). Each event then becomes a conscious choice to be happy. Then those choices can be woven into the fabric of everyday moments – stolen glances, shared dreams, waking up, next breath, great meal, walk in the park, or finally even the bittersweet acceptance of letting go someone in a divorce or death.

Gandhian Values

The bass thumped through Gauri's living room walls, shaking her once-serene evening. It was Susan's infamous barbecue again, loud and lively as always. Gauri, a devout follower of Gandhian ideals, had tolerated these parties, telling herself to "turn the other cheek." Yet tonight, her tolerance felt strangely thin.

Then, a loud crack split the air. Gauri rushed outside, only to see the fence that separated her yard from Susan's party now lying in splinters—a casualty of someone's overzealous behavior.

The next morning, Susan appeared at her door, looking mildly apologetic. "Hey, Gauri," she said, glancing at the fallen fence, "about that fence. Seems it broke during the party. I'll call a contractor and get it fixed. We can split the cost for repairs."

Gauri's carefully constructed edifice of tolerance crumbled. Anger, hot and sharp, pricked at her. Not only had the constant noise disrupted her peace, but now she was expected to contribute to fixing their mess! "Split the cost?" she echoed, her voice trembling. "It was your party, your guests who broke it! This is a blatant disregard for my property."

Susan's face tightened slightly, but she held her ground. "Look, I understand it's frustrating. But accidents happen, and I wouldn't have had the party if I thought it would cause damage," she said, almost as if expecting Gauri to let it go.

When Susan left, Gauri was left simmering in a mix of anger and guilt. Had her tolerance turned her into a doormat? She felt conflicted, unable to find the balance between her Gandhian ideals and her growing resentment.

Lost in this internal battle, Gauri felt trapped. Anger on one side fighting with her values on the other. She grew up in a simple middle-class family from rural Madhya Pradesh, having topped her engineering, moved here to do her master's and was working in a tech startup. Her upbringing was based on few values passed on by her parents.

And now the conflict did not seem fair. Why doesn't the anger subside by itself if values are to be held sacrosanct? She did not have an answer.

Seeking clarity, she called her mother early the next morning, knowing she'd be awake. "Ma," she began, "I'm not sure what to do. Technically, the fence is a shared responsibility. But it was Susan's party. She might say the fence was already weakened by last week's rains. She could easily talk her way out of this."

Her mother's voice was calm but firm. "Gauri, be clear with her. It was her fault, and she should take responsibility."

"But, Ma," Gauri hesitated, "it's just a fence—only a few thousand dollars. Why spoil my relationship with Susan over this? I could just split the cost and move on, but…"

"But what?" her mother pressed gently.

Gauri sighed, feeling vulnerable. "If I take that path, Ma, I'll feel angry at myself. I'm torn. I don't know what the right thing to do is."

Her mother paused before answering. "Do you remember the story I told you when you were young? The one about the sage and the snake?"

Gauri's brows knit together as she tried to recall.

"Let me remind you," her mother continued. "There was once a venomous snake that terrorized a village. When the villagers begged a sage to help, he commanded the snake to stop harming people. The snake agreed and became peaceful. But the next day, the villagers, seeing it as harmless, attacked it. The sage, seeing the snake bloodied and hurt, asked why it hadn't defended itself. The snake replied, 'You told me not to harm them, so I didn't.' To which the sage cried, 'O foolish snake, I told you not to bite. I never told you not to hiss and protect yourself!'"

Gauri's felt her feet an inch above the floor. A lightbulb went on inside her. Gandhian values, rooted in *Dharma*, did not advocate for blind tolerance. *Dharma*, she realized, was dynamic, adapting to the situation. It was not set it stone or word. It was, at best fluid and depended on the context. Turning the other cheek was not necessarily the right way to avoid unhappiness. Confrontation for a just cause was *dharma*. And, not picking up the cudgels at that time was *adharma*.

Was my espoused value of tolerance because I am fearful? She thought.

After a night's rest, Gauri knew her next steps. She approached Susan with a calm, steady resolve. "Susan," she began, "I understand accidents happen. But ignoring the consequences isn't the answer. We both need to be responsible here."

Susan looked surprised by Gauri's tone. "So…what are you suggesting?" she asked, cautiously.

"I'm suggesting that we split the repair cost," Gauri replied, "but given the circumstances, I'll cover 25%, and you'll take on the remaining 75%. And, Susan, I would appreciate it if your parties from now on were within a reasonable noise level. And if there's any future damage, I'd expect you to cover it fully."

Susan hesitated, then nodded, clearly relieved there was no hostility. "That sounds fair, Gauri. I'll make sure it's taken care of."

As she walked back to her quiet garden, Gauri felt at peace, having stood up for herself without compromising her values. She realized now that tolerance and non-violence weren't just about "turning the other cheek." They meant choosing the right path, sometimes one of quiet firmness, to protect her peace and uphold her values.

Gauri stood a little taller that day. She had found a way to protect her space, her peace, and her values. Non-violence, or tolerance, she understood, wasn't just about turning the other cheek; it was about using her voice, her reason, to create a space where peace and understanding could flourish. It was about adhering to the true essence of *Dharma* – acting in accordance with what was right, in that specific context.

Universal values like tolerance, non-violence, love and compassion are never absolute, but relative in nature. She sat in her quiet garden, the sound of the birds singing was no longer drowned out by loud music. She had found a way to hold onto her Gandhian values, adapted and strengthened by the wisdom of an ancient sage and a wounded snake.

Raghupathi Raghava Rajaram

The air crackled with nervous energy backstage at the local temple competition. Children were prepped by their moms and dads for the talent show. Some choose to sing a song, few play an instrument or show off a few classical dance moves – *Bharatanatyam, Kuchipudi, Kathak…*

These are the times that she hated but had to go because Rohan wanted to. As she soaked in the American culture, she had slowly found less and less time to for *stuff,* as she called it, beyond work, work, and work, occasionally family chores. And Bala was worse. He never stepped into a temple the past dozen years they lived here. Even when they holidayed in India, it was always about exploring some forest range, mountains, kayaking and similar such adventure sports. He was a converted atheist, who found no need for God in his life. Everything he needed to run his startup, his home, his relationships – wife, son, parents, friends, and in-laws back in India always was an outcome of meticulous planning, applying rational thought and expecting commensurate outcomes. Madhushree, dressed in a shimmering sari, fidgeted with her bangles. She wished Bala would join on these occasions to the temple at least to provide her moral support. But….

Her six-year-old son, Rohan, stood beside her, his eyes wide with excitement. He clutched a crumpled paper with a song scrawled in messy English, a song she'd taught him with pride. She remembered it as if it were yesterday, having sung this on *Gandhi Jayanti* during her school days. "*Raghupathi Raghava Raja Ram,*" it began, the rest a garbled mix of Hindi and English that rhymed, at least, phonetically.

One by one, contestants took the stage, children in colorful costumes, belting out traditional *bhajans* with surprising clarity. Then came Rohan's turn. He took a deep breath and launched into his "song." He had a good voice, great enthusiasm and courage to get in front of forty kids plus about double the number of proud parents, in bedazzling *desi* dresses – *sarees, kurtis, salwar kameez, ghagra choli* to show off their *desi'ness.* When he finished, there was an awkward silence. The judges exchanged bewildered looks. A polite smile from one judge was all they got.

He did not win the prize. Later, as they walked home, Madhushree's heart felt heavy. Rohan, sensing her disappointment, kicked a pebble down the sidewalk. "Did I not sing well, *Amma*?"

"No, no, you sang beautifully," she assured him, forcing a smile. But shame simmered in her gut. *Why had she felt embarrassed?*

Pulling out her phone, she searched for the song, "*Raghupathi Raghava.*" Was there a mistake in her teaching? It was a beautiful composition that Gandhi-*ji* had created. For twelve years, she had sung this every Oct 2nd at school. The melodious tune had washed over her, the words, powerful and poetic, igniting a spark within. The YouTube also showed her some other version of the song, entitled the 'Original

Raghupathi Raghava Rajaram[12]. Curiosity enveloped her and she played that song. As she listened, shame morphed into anger. She searched for the lyrics and meaning of the original and found it soon. *Saala! Macaulay, tu iska kaaran tha?* She felt pissed at the education system that had failed her, anger at herself for neglecting her heritage. In the name of secularism and unity, Gandhi had created a version, that had become the default.

That night, she held Rohan close, tears welling up in her eyes. "*Beta*," she said, her voice thick with emotion, "I made a mistake. The song you sang… it wasn't quite right."

Rohan' eyes widened. "But you taught me, *Amma*."

"And I was wrong," she confessed. "But from now on, we'll learn together, okay?"

She spent the next few weeks with Rohan, rediscovering the song in original and naturally, her rich heritage. They sang together *bhajans* in their original form, the language rolling off their tongues, albeit imperfectly. They read stories from authentic sources, unadulterated by the filters of a foreign system.

As Rohan stood on the stage again, this time at a different temple competition, his voice rang out, clear and confident. He sang the full original version of "*Raghupathi Raghava*," the meaning resonating with every syllable. This time, there was no awkward silence. There was thunderous applause.

---

12   https://learncarnaticmusicblog.wordpress.com/2022/04/10/
     raghupathi-raghava-rajaram-original-lyrics-original-ram-dhun/

Madhushree beamed, her heart overflowing with pride. It wasn't just Rohan's victory; it was their victory. A victory not just in a competition, but in reclaiming their heritage, a heritage that had been lost, forgotten, then found again, piece by melodious piece. She knew this was the very sincere beginning of a discovery. The deep imprints and scars of Macaulay's legacy will remain, a constant reminder, but with each song learned, each story read, each temple visited that nonsense will grew fainter, replaced by the vibrant tapestry of their true Indian identity.

Back home, she rummaged through her childhood books, dusty relics of her Indian education. They were filled with sanitized versions of epics, sanitized versions of *bhajans*, sanitized versions of her own culture. She decided to throw them away. Macaulay's English education system, she realized bitterly, had become a double-edged sword. It had surely allowed them to excel in the new world but had also robbed them of a deep connection to their heritage.

"Part of the blame also lay with us too." She thought. It was a fact at that instant when the memory resurfaced. *Her grandmother, defying her parents' modernizing ways, had taught her many bhajans in their original, evocative Hindi and Sanskrit. But Madhushree, embarrassed by the "backwardness" of it all, had not wanted to sing those archaic ones, and instead preferring to sing the sanitized English versions in school.*

Her thoughts fast forwarded. *What has been done is done. Now, she had the chance to do things differently for Rohan. She would make sure he understood both the richness of his heritage and the modern world they lived in. She would teach him to carry his culture with pride, unashamed and unfiltered, so he could feel both American and Indian without compromise.*

Sanatana Dharma is Not a Diet Plan

Naveen stood in the bustling crowd of the Jagannatha Rath Yatra, watching the chariots sway through the streets, their vibrant colors blending into a sea of devotion. Born in coastal Orissa but raised in the United States, Naveen had recently started reconnecting with his Sanatana Dharma roots. Yet, a nagging doubt persisted: could he truly consider himself a Hindu if he enjoyed the occasional burger?

Back in his ancestral village, fish and prawn curries had been a staple. Here in America, however, he'd noticed a strong association between vegetarianism and "true" devotion, and it made him question if his own dietary preferences could coexist with his faith. Spotting the temple priest nearby, Naveen decided to ask..

"Panditji," he began, his voice barely a whisper above the chanting, "I'm trying to embrace my faith, but… I love non-vegetarian food. Is there a place for me in *Hinduism*?"

The priest, his gaze twinkling with understanding, ushered Naveen into a quieter corner. "Ah, the eternal question," he chuckled. "A great teacher once said, *Hinduism is not a diet plan*. There are no prescriptions. During the *Mahabharata* times, and surely earlier ages as well, people ate meat. There are *slokas* in *Aranya Parva* when Yudhishtira says to a bunch of *sannyasis*, while embarking to the forest that they will live in the forest for 12 years by eating roots, fruits, and flesh (*aamisha*)." He explained. "The principle is not about banning food types—it's about living in alignment with 'least harm'".

"And, what about the guilt of killing an animal? People don't feel guilty eating plants though." Naveen pressed, a concern he'd often wrestled with.

"*Sanatana Dharma* is a living religion, with changes in form and function but never to the core principle /substance. For example, in *Vedic* times, the popular 'Gods' were *Surya* (sun), *Indra* (king of Gods or king of rain) and *Soma* (the plant associated with the Moon, from which the mystical 'soma-ras' was extracted). As time progressed, the forms of the Gods changed. We pray now to Krishna, Rama, Ganesha etc., who were never in the pantheon during those times, but the underlying 'principle' that we pray to, has not changed. Similarly, eating habits can change over time, but the principle of *ahimsa* does not change. From the *Vedic* culture to now, the principle remains, but the civilizations adapt to eating what is convenient, available, nutritious, local. Yet, they must follow the principle of 'least harm', not 'no harm'. "

He added. "Around the time of Buddha, and probably due to the influence of Buddhism, the concept of *ahimsa* extended to animals." *Panditji's* wisdom flowed in bursts like the *theertha* he was offering to those in the line after the evening prayer.

Naveen knew that asking *Panditji* about the inherent conflict of *ahimsa* – non injury /nonviolence was a rabbit hole that he did not want to take. But maybe he guessed what was on Naveen's mind and continued. "*ahimsa* does not mean **non**injury or **non**violence. It is a path of least harm. It is impossible to live in this earth without *himsa,* the opposite of *ahimsa.* When you get some time, read the story of *Vyadha Gita* in *Mahabharata.* In that, a learned *Brahmin* is given a talk on *dharma* by a butcher! He logically explains that even eating plants, seeds involve *himsa.* The act of tilling the soil itself kills insects & other beings who have made the soil as their homes. Moreover, he also clarifies that suicide is not the way out as that is *himsa* towards oneself."

Naveen felt something shift within him, a glimmer of clarity. "Panditji," he asked, "so does that mean those who avoid meat are somehow 'better' in their devotion?"

Panditji smiled. A smile said it all to Naveen.

"*Panditji.* Who then can eat meat and who should not? Are there any guidelines?"

"The principle of *ahimsa* when understood well will help you with your answer. Do you want me to? It could take time. Can you meet me after the evening *aarti?*" *Panditji* requested him, eager to share what he knows, while at the same time, knew it was closing time and the final prayers and worship of the day should be offered to the Lord.

With a takeaway packet in hand – *prasad,* he waited for *Panditji* to finish the final tasks in the sanctum sanctorum.

"Only humans have the ability /faculty of making choices. Because of this superpower, only we can decide what constitutes least harm. We are on the top of the food chain. And plants are at the bottom of the food chain. Practically speaking which of the two options – eating something at the lower end of the food chain vs. near the top of food chain causes least harm? Daily there is a choice between various options in the food chain, and if we exercise the freewill properly we have, then what is least harm is easy to understand. It is easy to decide, I think." said *Panditji*.

And then he added new-age perspective which hit Naveen like a thunderbolt. In his newly minted role as an ambassador of sustainability at his company, this was a unique insight that eating plants was better, that he had read about in one of the United Nations latest reports on food scarcity and environment. He always had this suspicion that the big meat companies hid the truth well about how the final packaged product in the shelves that we buy, had been produced.

"In these days where we are concerned about environment, if we change our food habits, then it surely helps in lower carbon emissions. When our choices are as close as possible to plants in the food chain, the lower the emissions are. What we eat, Naveen, does shape us in subtle ways. *Tamasic* food – meat in excess – can cloud the mind, making it difficult to grasp the deeper truths of the Upanishads."

Pausing a few seconds, *Panditji* continued.

"And your coastal roots, Naveen?" the priest added, a knowing glint in his eyes. "Just like the *Konkan* people by the sea, being *Odiya* and enjoying fish is perfectly natural. Food is a function of your geography, your culture as well."

Naveen grinned, feeling a rush of relief. He wasn't an outsider or an imposter. He could embrace his heritage and his diet without feeling like he was betraying his faith. The Rath Yatra had been a grand spectacle of devotion, but for him, it had also become a journey of personal rediscovery, one where his faith could coexist with both his roots and his choices.

Uncork the Wine

Mukund stared at the stubborn wine bottle, his grip tightening around the corkscrew as laughter and the celebratory clinking of glasses drifted from the living room. His startup's Series C funding had gone through—a massive win, one worth celebrating with champagne. Yet, here he was, alone in the kitchen, grappling with the bottle, his nerves an odd mix of accomplishment and anxiety. In twenty years, he'd grown used to Anjali handling things like this: choosing the wine, the menu, knowing what everyone would enjoy. She'd convinced him to splurge this time on the best wine—and even, as a rare exception, non-veg dishes.

But tonight felt different. Mukund had always been a teetotaler, a habit he'd clung to since moving to the US. He wasn't thrilled with the idea of entertaining with alcohol but had accepted it as a part of their American life. He knew Anjali had adapted to the culture in ways he hadn't. She was shy and reserved in India, but here, she'd flourished. She'd become a connoisseur of wine—a hobby that had surprised him at first, yet he'd made peace with it over time.

Life after moving to the US had been a whirlwind for Mukund. Anjali, a shy, bookish girl back in India, had blossomed so much that her friends called her transformation no less magical than a caterpillar turning into a butterfly. She came from a very traditional *desi* family. She was brought up with lots of restrictions – what they ate & drank at home. They say that words have special meaning in families. In theirs, 'drinking' was associated either water or *chai* naturally and *nimbu-paani, lassi, chaach* or *Roohafza* during summers. She married Mukund and within a week they were in US. She had found a job in a very small startup where the CEO threw weekly parties for all his staff. Soon, unknowingly to herself, she knew her cabernets, pinots, full-bodied, rose's, whites & reds, dessert, sparkling, merlots, syrah and probably two dozen more. She knew them not just from the names, but from the smell, taste and feel.

"Need help, Dad?" Diya's voice pulled him from his thoughts. She reached for the bottle and, with an expert twist of the corkscrew, popped it open.

He looked at her, taken aback. "How did you…?"

Diya smiled, a hint of amusement in her eyes. "It's normal here, Dad. Parties, college, you know…"

The word "normal" struck him. He forced a smile, retreating to the living room where colleagues congratulated him with their glasses raised high. But something felt off, a growing discomfort he couldn't quite shake.

Later, as the last guest departed, Mukund braced himself for the inevitable conversation with Anjali. He approached carefully. "Diya shouldn't be drinking," he began, his tone controlled but his disapproval clear.

Anjali's face tightened. "Mukund, she's an adult—or almost. This is normal here. Let her live."

The word stung him again. "Normal," he muttered. "I'm sure this started earlier than I thought."

Anjali sighed, the exasperation clear in her voice. "On her sixteenth birthday, I offered her a small drink. She's grown up in a different culture, Mukund. She can't be like us, drinking water every time her friends raise a toast."

"But we're not so different," he replied, trying to stay calm. "Your background, our upbringing—it was the same. We grew up just a few doors apart, Anjali. We never even imagined drinking." They were childhood friends, who fell in love and married.

Anjali was upset.

"Don't tell me how to raise my child. I am her mother. I know her better. She can't be like you, drinking water every time we hang out with friends."

"This isn't Rampur," she continued. "We must fit in here, be part of this society. You know that as much as I do."

Mukund paced, feeling the walls close in. "I'm in Silicon Valley, Anjali. This is my second startup, and I think I'm doing fine without drinking or golf. This is a meritocracy. Success isn't tied to a drink in hand. I can't believe you encouraged Diya. How can you corrupt a young mind and make her drink?" He was terribly upset that Anjali was the protagonist of this *natak*.

Their words volleyed back and forth until a heavy silence fell between them. They both knew this argument, like others before it, wouldn't resolve anything. Diya would continue to drink. Anjali would accept it. And Mukund, reluctant and conflicted, would have to make peace with it.

As he lay in bed later, Mukund thought about his father's words on raising children: *It's the hardest thing you'll ever do.* And perhaps his father had been right. Mukund believed in giving Diya freedom, but a part of him wished he'd set clearer boundaries earlier. He just hoped that she would always understand the value of those boundaries—even if they felt confining now.

Hindu Bible

Fourteen-year-old Sumana, a second-generation Indian American, bit her lip in curiosity. Sarah, her best friend, had just declared, "I read the Bible every night, helps me understand what it means to be a Christian."

Sumana knew that Sarah goes to church with her parents and little brother every Sunday and prays. Her family was different she knew. She was brought up in a secular home. Her parents had decided it was best if they did not mix their faith in her upbringing. In all her life, she had never been to a temple. Of course, she would not remember when she was taken to the temple for her *annaprasna,* the first 'solid food' feeding ceremony. At the insistence of her grandparents, her mom and dad had reluctantly taken the then few months baby Sumana to the local temple. She had pictures of that function. But the idea of a religious text sparked a simple question in Sumana's mind. She knew little about her own cultural past. When she got back home, she asked. "Mom," she asked tentatively, "What's the, like, *Hindu* Bible?"

All her parents had told her was that she was born into a Hindu family. That too, just a few years ago when she had to do an assignment for school about heritage and culture. She had researched about festivals celebrated, clothes Hindus wear, food they eat and a bit about temples and put together an impressive presentation.

Her mother, bustling around the kitchen, paused. "The *Bhagavad Gita, beta*," she replied, a hint of uncertainty in her voice. And, truth be told, the *Gita* was a book she'd never cracked open herself. "I have a copy of it in the shelf. It was your *thatha's* copy and he had given it to me before he died." She added.

Intrigued, Sumana found a well-worn copy tucked away on a high shelf. Skipping through the first few pages, she delved straight into the first chapter of the book. An hour later she was totally confused.

The opening scene depicted a battlefield, Arjuna, a warrior prince, filled with doubt about fighting his own kin. *He was dead right, Wars kill. They destroy families. Cost of war is very high. Look at the Israel-Hamas war or the Russia-Ukraine.* thought Sumana. Images of gore, war machines, propaganda, protests across the US against war, reminders of the destruction the two world wars caused all flashed through her mind. And Arjuna's arguments why he should not fight this war was all valid. It totally resonated with her.

But then came Krishna's voice, urging him to not drop his weapons and fight. For what? Krishna was talking of some elusive *dharma*. Morals? Ethics? *One can't stick to ethics when life is in danger. How can this be the 'Hindu Bible'? It is an instigation to war. Krishna is brainwashing Arjuna to fight. So sickening.*

Sumana's stomach churned. This book wasn't a message of peace! It was an incitement to war!

Days turned into weeks as Sumana wrestled with the text. Weren't the teachings of Gandhi, India's freedom fighter, rooted in non-violence? How could this *holy* book advocate for bloodshed? Didn't she read somewhere that millions died in the Mahabharata war?

She googled and instantly found her answer: 11+8 *akshauhini* [13] of armies on *Kaurava + Pandava* sides perish. A few more searches on what this term meant, and some basic math was staggering. A mountain of a figure showed up on her excel sheet: 3,936,600. And the narrative she remembered from the Amar Chitra Katha stories her mom narrated was: *all male except for the five Pandava brothers and a few more, from both the warring cousin camps had died. The women were widowed and children left fatherless.* It does seem miniscule compared to the estimated 80 million deaths during World War 2. But if she adjusted [14] for the population increase in the past 5500 years, it was estimated to be about 5 million! So, it was indeed the destruction of entire human race at that time.

All because of *this* book! How can this be called *the Bible of Hindus?* Why did Krishna, who claimed he was God, choose to give such a terrible advice? Was he such a powerful demagogue or was Arjuna so gullible?

For an entire week what she discovered did not sit well with her. She neither ate nor drank. She was depressed. She feigned

---

13   Adi Parva 2.15.23 : 1 chariot:1 elephant:3 horses:5 infantry per *akshauhini.* https://en.wikipedia.org/wiki/Akshauhini#:~:text=An%20akshauhi ni%20(Sanskrit:%20%E0%A4%85%E0%A4%95%E0%A5%8D%E0% A4%B7%E0%A5%8C%E0%A4%B9%E0%A4%BF%E0%A4%A3%E0 %A5%80%20ak%E1%B9%A3auhi%E1%B9%87%C4%AB,digits%20 add%20up%20to%2018.

14   https://www.worldometers.info/world-population/world-population-by-year/

sickness and stopped going to school. Not wanting to see Sarah was another reason. What will she say?

Fortunately, that weekend, her grandmother was arriving from India. It was a welcome change for her to have someone at home, with both mom and dad off to their work all day long. Her grandma took her first trip overseas since grandpa died a decade ago. Mom had taken turns to go visit her once a year after grandpa's death, but Sumana did not visit India even once. But she had spent enough FaceTime with her, and they were not strangers to each other. *Au contraire*, they were thick friends.

"Isn't the Gita supposed to be a wise? " Sumana questioned, frustration lacing her words. "Why does it tell people to go to war?"

Her grandmom, a gentle soul of quiet wisdom, smiled. "Sumana, the Gita isn't a simple manual. It's about finding purpose and doing the right thing, even when faced with the hardest choice."

She continued explaining the context of the war to Sumana better. It was a fight against cunning *Duryodhana* and his brothers and his evil well-wishers. They had illegally usurped the land that *Pandavas* had and even molested their cherished wife *Draupadi* in the full light of all courtiers in the *sabha*. For thirteen years after the ill-fated game of dice, these five princes lived like hermits in forest, vowing to return to their kingdom afterwards. But when the promised kingdom was not returned to them, they had no choice but to declare war. And it was not a hasty declaration either. *Yudhishtira* tried to compromise, and he asked for just five small villages. But his evil-minded cousin, and son of the blind king *Dhritarashtra, Duryodhana* declared they would not even get land the area of five sewing needles!

"But Arjuna, on seeing the enormous army from both sides arraigned to fight with each other, develops cold feet. He wants to run away to the forests." Says grandma.

"That is when Krishna teaches him what his duty was."

Seeing the quizzical look on Sumana's face, she continued.

"Everybody has a role to play in this universe. Your parents have responsibilities towards you and imagine what would happen if they abdicated that? You too have responsibilities. If you don't study hard, what would happen to your future? Similarly, think of the five *Pandavas*. They had a role as kings to protect and nurture their kingdom. Irrespective of their likes or dislikes. Or emotions of empathy."

Still the creases of confusion did not erase easily. The patient grandma shared a bit more.

"Arjuna (& his brothers') were kings. They had the mindset of able and just administrators. And they fought for what was justifiably theirs. They even wanted to negotiate to avoid war and in return accept smaller piece of land. They took a flexible position but the other side did not budge. Then they had no choice but to fight. Krishna's counsel to the hesitant warrior was to be detached and act. Doing one's duty without succumbing to hatred or fear. Sure, war is violent and has terrible consequences, but Krishna taught *Arjuna* that he cannot avoid it because *(he) Arjuna did not like it.*"

Sumana listened intently. *Maybe*, she thought, *there was more to the story than she initially understood. Perhaps, the Gita wasn't a war manual, but a guide to navigating life's complexities.* She thought she heard the deeper message in her grandma's words – *duties, and doing them, doesn't matter whether we like to do them or not. That sounds like practical advice applicable even today!*

"Is it something like the surgeon refusing to amputate the patient's arm because the surgeon doesn't like bloodshed?" asked a curious Sumana.

"That's a great example. The surgeon's job is to save the patient. If amputation was the only way forward, then does she have a choice at all on what he should do?" The grandma smiled, admiring her *jigar ka tukda*.

"The first chapter and half of the *Gita* is the set up. It is the context from which we must learn the message. And, you did not go beyond the first few pages, right?" a smile and a wink from her grandma increased the slight discomfort and embarrassment she felt of making judgements even before she did her own work!

Thankfully it was summertime soon and over the course of the few weeks in summer, they together explored different interpretations of the Gita. Finally, Sumana learned of its focus on self-knowledge, control of mind and sense organs and the power of right choices. She leant that it was all about fulfilling one's role with integrity, even when faced with an impossible choice.

And Arjuna did face a terrible choice – kill his kinsmen and win the war with no one to rule afterwards or chicken out and regret all his life while facing ridicule from everyone, even after his death.

What was the duty of a warrior to do then? What choice he had to choose?

The black and white of her initial understanding transformed into a spectrum of gray. The Gita, she realized, wasn't a call to violence, but a call to action – to fight for what's right, even if the battle is internal.

Then her grandma asked her a question she never thought about.

"Do you know what your name means?"

"Nope." Prompt came the reply.

"Sumana means one with an excellent mind. *Su* (meaning excellent) is prefixed to *mana* (the one who has a mind). It is your excellent mind that is prompting you to be curious, to learn" she said, leaving Sumana a bit embarrassed.

Aryan Invasion

Twelve-year-old Anjali slammed her history textbook shut, a frown creasing her forehead. "*Amma*, this doesn't make sense!" she declared, her voice laced with frustration. Her grandmother looked up from her prayer beads, her kind eyes crinkling at the corners. "What is it, my Anjali?"

Anjali shoved the book toward her grandmother, frustration tightening her voice. "It says the Aryans were fair-skinned people who invaded India and took over. But, Nani, people here have always looked like us!"

Nani chuckled softly, the gentle sound easing Anjali's tension. "Ah, the Aryan invasion theory. Many young minds, just like yours, have puzzled over it for years."

Anjali's frown deepened. "But it's in the textbook, Nani – isn't that history?"

Her grandmother scanned through the book. A picture of Devi Jagadambika temple in Khajuraho and below that picture was a timeline, attributed to National Geographic, about when the early India civilization began. She observed what the kids were being taught! As she read she few pages from the text book, she was appalled and mentally underlined a few sentences that struck her as misleading history.

c.3000 B.C. was supposedly when the Indian civilization began and c.1500 B.C was when Aryans arrive in India. The basic principles of what is known today as Hinduism were already formulated by 1500 B.C. They are to be found in the four Vedas. The Aryans believed in many deities who controlled the forces of nature and governed society. We know about Aryan religion from their sacred hymns and poetry, especially their epics, or long poems.

The Aryans came from central Asia where they raised and herded animals. The Aryans were not a race or ethnic group. Some historians believe that the Aryans were part of a larger group they refer to as Indo-Europeans. The Indo-Europeans all spoke similar languages. Some migrated south to India and Iran. Others went west to Europe.

The Aryans bring change. Their technology improved farming in India. They also brought a new language to India. As nomads, they had no written language, but in India they developed a written language called Sanskrit. Now the sacred songs, poems and prayers that Aryans had known for many centuries could be written down.

The Aryans created a caste system that separated Indians into groups. One of the results of the Aryan arrival in India was the development of a caste system. A caste is a social group that someone is born into and cannot leave.

She thought, *I should have underlined everything* ☹.

Then she saw the much-maligned hierarchical pyramid with *Brahmins* on the top, followed by *Kshatriyas, Vaisyas, Sudras.*

And interestingly, the book depicted *Pariahs*, another group below *Sudras!*

More lies follow that about caste system. The textbook insinuates that such a system was created probably because of skin color. She thought – *Are American school textbooks conflating the race conflict here in US and applying it to ancient India?*

And then more blatant lies followed. *When a man from a prominent family died, his wife was expected to leap into flames. This practice was called 'suttee'.* Finally in a grand reveal, the textbook attributes that Aryans created Hinduism!

Nani patted the space beside her on the rug. "Come, sit with me, Anjali. Let's talk about history, but the kind passed down through generations, the kind that is composed in different musical meters, learnt and shared from one generation to another. "

As Anjali settled down, *Nani* began, her voice warm and soothing. "The word 'Aryan' comes from *Sanskrit*, Anjali. It doesn't mean a race or skin color. It just means 'noble', 'respected' 'or cultured.'""

Anjali's eyes widened. "But the book says..."

"The book tells one story, child," *Nani* interrupted gently, "but our scriptures tell another. Look at the *Ramayana*, the story of Rama, the ideal king. He's described as an *Arya*, a noble prince."

Anjali thought for a moment. "So, the Aryans weren't invaders? They were just... good people?"

Nani smiled. "Perhaps there were migrations, people moving from one place to another. But it wasn't a violent conquest. Think of it like rivers merging, their waters mixing and flowing together. That's how our civilization grew, with different cultures enriching each other."

She continued. "Your textbook says that *Sanskrit* was a written language. It is not true. Our traditions were passed down orally. *Gurukul* system of education was the only way through which a *guru* transmits what (s)he knew – philosophy, morality, ethics, prayers etc., to their students. And it was done in *Sanskrit*! Even today there are people who memorize the entire *Vedas*. Those people in our ancient times had great capacity to learn, retain in memory and recite, quote contextually and share. This was the very reason why our culture was not destroyed despite multiple invasions over the course of ages."

What her grandmother said seems to make sense. But more doubts prevail in her mind. Anjali flipped through the textbook again, her eyes scanning the pages with newfound skepticism. "But what about the Indus Valley people? Did they just disappear?"

"Not at all," Nani said. "Their knowledge, their traditions, they all became part of the fabric of our *Sanatana Dharma*. The concept of *Dharma* itself, doing one's duty, transcends skin color or origin."

She let that sink in. Anjali did not probably understand the import of what she said. She let it pass. Then continued. "The textbook seems to spout nonsense about caste! Especially the part about *being born into a particular caste and can never leave.* Portuguese colonizers, and later the British colonizers created and perpetrated the current social system called 'caste' in India. *Bhagavad Gita* says that grouping of people has been existing since time immemorial. And it is not restricted to India geography alone. Wherever there are people, these four groups exist. The concept is more like *having the qualifications for a job that one needs to do in corporate America today.* Importantly, it also says that it is based NOT on birth, but based on an individual's mindset, or mental qualities and the type of work they are most likely to prefer. When such a classification exists, it automatically paves way for a person to 'move' from one group to another, as their mindset changes and their natural preference to the type of work changes."

She noticed Anjali was already drawn into the complex topic that most people misunderstand. Grandmother took a pause. She accepted that the society today has been divided by 'caste', which was an unfortunate outcome of our recent colonized history. No doubt certain selfish individuals across generations perpetrated the 'caste' system the way we know it today, because it served their interests.

But grandmothers are wise. They are so because they have been told about our ancient culture through stories like Mahabharata and Ramayana. She knew that in ancient India, work mobility was limited, and a child took the family profession as their own. And she also knew that in Mahabharata, there are several instances of individuals born as *sudras* have been acknowledged by even learned *brahmins* as well as people born into the *brahmin, kshatriya* and *Vaisya* families. She even had a story ready to tell Anjali – the story of *DharmaVyadha*[15]!

But Anjali seems to have moved on to another question that bothered her.

"So, *Nani*, what should I believe?" she asked, her voice small.

Nani squeezed her hand. "Believe in what resonates with your heart, Anjali. But most importantly, question everything. Read widely, delve into our ancient texts, and learn the true meaning of words like *Arya*."

Anjali looked at her grandmother, a newfound respect sparkling in her eyes. History, she realized, wasn't just about memorizing dates and events. Neither was it about accepting everything anyone or any book says, including the school textbooks. It was about piecing together the puzzle, questioning narratives, and understanding the rich tapestry of her own heritage.

Anjali's mom, Revati suddenly realized that the *dal* was getting burnt on the stove. She had been eavesdropping on the grandmother-granddaughter conversation that she forgot to

---

15   In *Mahabharata,* A highly learned *brahmana* goes to a butcher *sudra* to learn about what is *dharma, karma,* right action, wrong actions. The discourse between them is popularly known as *vyadha* (butcher) *gita* (discourse). This story illustrates two things – a teacher can be anyone, doing any work and that all professions, however demeaning it may sound from a societal point of view, are worthy of the respect they deserve. See the introduction to this book for a better context of this story.

what was on the stove! That night after Anjali slept, she went into her mother's room.

"*Amma,* what you shared with Anjali today was beautiful. I did not know this. Our children are being fed poison at school; it seems. This is intellectually dishonest. If I were to go to school and lodge a complaint, will you help me build a proper case?" she asked, a deep embarrassment slowly coming up in her words as she spoke. In her heart, she recalled the incident when she came back after joining protestors urging government for more reservations for 'backward classes'. She was woken then and continued to be one, doing what she felt was right and just. She had not wanted to listen to any of what her mom was saying and was in a bubble. And her mom had told her angrily then – *jab tumhara baccha ho jayega, tab teri aankh khulegi*[16].

Her mother could only smile now.

Call it by whatever name – *grand happening* or *circle of life.*

---

16   When you have a child, your eyes will open (to the reality).

Cake Ya Ayush-homam?

Akash stared at the vibrant children's book in Hindi, the squiggly letters a foreign language to his eyes. The evening's event made him pick up that instead of the English storybook that he usually reads Anya.

Anya was nicely tucked in her bed. Eyes rolling, and at times drooping, tired from the party. She was expecting her usual perhaps – a lullaby to finally go off into her dreamland.

They had just celebrated her first birthday grandly. All their friends had come for the party. It was an enjoyable way of meeting up their friends' families and children. Friends become family here when family and relatives are far away back in India. Bonds must be created; relationships must be strengthened, and all of this takes time. Time was exactly what people don't have. Work, eat, drink, sleep and work is the virtuous cycle of life in America. At times of extreme homesickness or despondency, it was called *rat race*. Taking time to host these occasional parties, or frisbee outings, before Akash and Priya had Anya was the binding glue that kept things going together for all.

The cake was huge. Barbie was still popular, but PAW Patrol was more in vogue with new parents. Anya's cake was shaped like Skye.

As Priya blew the candle and Akash cut the cake, everyone sang the popular refrain, Happy Birthday.

As Akash was going around the party, making sure that everyone got the *samosas*, cake and fries, John's mom asked him. "How would you celebrate birthdays back in India?" John was one of his high school friends. Their family had moved from the UK around the same time Akash's parents relocated to the US. They had become good friends from day one. Yet, this was the first time he was meeting his parents.

An innocent question. But that bothered him. He did not know why.

And now, as he looked at the Hindi script, he realized that he was an illiterate. He spoke, read, and thought in English. Although he tried to learn Hindi as a kid, the memories faded fast no sooner they landed in US. His parents sang to him in Hindi and perhaps those were hidden in some cold storage of his mind, unretrievable without a key that he knew not what it was. Akash yearned to sing her a song in his mother tongue, but his own Hindi was a rusty relic of childhood visits to India.

Guilt gnawed at him. He prided himself on being multicultural – a comfortable mix of Indian heritage and American upbringing. His idea of being multicultural was just being inclusive. Like celebrating Thanksgiving with turkey and mashed potatoes and Diwali with firecrackers and *gulab-jamoons*.

He felt like an imposter.

Priya, sensing his turmoil, sat beside him. Akash shared his imposter syndrome with her.

"A lot has changed since we left India, Akash," she said gently. "Our parents cooked with instinct, not cookbooks. We learned philosophy through stories, not classrooms. We have forgotten all. Can't blame ourselves, can we? We are in a new place; new culture and we need to adapt to this place." Priya was a practical person, not giving into sentimentalities unlike him.

Akash nodded. Yet he had a sleepless night.

The following weekend, he drove to his parents' place. They lived a few hundred miles away. Their parents did not know how Indians celebrated birthday – the traditional style. They were the 60's generation when English education was most sought after to get a good job. We can't blame them; they had succeeded both financially and socially. After retiring at sixty, his dad continued to consult for the company he had founded decades ago.

"Let's ask the priest at the temple when we go there next week?" suggested his mom.

"The traditional style of birthday celebrations is called *Ayush-homam*." The priest from their local temple said. Priya and Akash listened to him intently while Anya was fast asleep blissfully unaware of the chimes of the temple bell being rung by the regular stream of devotees.

"In traditional Indian culture, everything is a prayer. Not a wish. We don't wish for long life. *Ayush*[17]-*homam* is a traditional prayer fire ritual where we pray for long life. It's

---

17   *Aayus,* the *Sanskrit* words means the reminder of the life. *Homa* is an oblation with fire.

fine if you blow the candle and cut the cake – nothing wrong with what we do here" he re-assured them.

The subtle difference between prayer and wish missed Akash. He pressed *Panditji.* "I did not understand the difference. Kindly explain."

"Wishes are like horses. They can go anywhere, everywhere. They have no bearing, and they need not fructify. But prayers have specific purpose. They are directed towards that Supreme Being who is the bestower of its results. Prayers have power because of this. It is a subtle difference but a deep philosophy of life." said *Panditji.*

A piece seemed to move in its right place in the entire jigsaw of understanding the complexity of a cultural heritage. But they were determined to learn. They promised to come back to him often and seek his counsel to understand better.

As Anya grew, Akash and Priya made several adjustments to their life. They were practical. They had limited time. And they focused on their careers too. So whatever was the time left after work, they tried to learn. They tried different cuisines from India, while not leaving out pasta, pizzas, and burgers. Anya liked them. Sometimes the food came out well, sometimes not. But they kept at it.

Akash called his mom one day and declared, "Mamma, I want to talk with you only in Hindi going forward." His mom was not surprised by this change. Soon, he started picking up broken Hindi. "*Toota-foota*" teased his *desi* cousin from Delhi! He started watching Bollywood movies to learn to speak Hindi. And his cousin appreciated him and egged him on.

"*Entertainment ka entertainment* without the guilt of wasting time. *Wah bhai, wah!* One shot two birds." He spoke.

"We wanted to raise Anya as bicultural kids, taking the best of India and America. Strange that we are learning a lot." He said to Priya one night.

"We have changed Akash. And that was the only way to raise a child bicultural. No amount of *telling* and *yelling* will work with Anya. She is almost five now and what I see is that she attempts her cute yoga poses because you practice yoga. And, she speaks Hindi because you do. Malayalam, because of me. She wears the *lehenga* and *bindi* when we go to the temple and is comfortable in that. She loves *Chota Bhim* as much as she likes Disney characters. And she LOVES stories from *Panchatantra.* She loves to travel to ancient temples in India as much as she likes to visit the national parks here. She likes her pasta, pizza too as much as she like the *Onam Sadya* on the banana leaf that we tried last time." She said.

"And we burnt the sweet dish." He remarked jokingly, yet lovingly. They both laughed.

"We have a lot to learn. Anya going from a year old to five was not that difficult. In the next ten years, as she develops both physically and emotionally, we need to ramp up our learning. The curiosity she has about both these cultures will get snubbed a bit by the friend circle around, and her changing priorities. We need to be patient and let her wander a bit before finding her roots. Our job is to plant those seeds firmly in her mind and water them regularly. That means, we need to change." She spoke.

"Karo Pahle, Kaho Peeche." Akash said, as he was reminded of the story of Ramakrishna Paramahamsa who would not advise a youngster not to eat sweets, because he was fond of sweets himself and had to wean himself off first before he advised that boy.

"I am also excited to discover new things about our culture. We have just skimmed the surface. *Panditji* was talking about the concept of *"Vasudhaiva Kutumbakam*[18]*"* and how would we implement it in our own lives matters more than telling her."

"While you worry about those big concepts Priya, I am more concerned about how we are going to celebrate her sixth birthday. Cake or *homam?"* he joked, remembering that Anya's birthday was coming up in a month. He knew that Priya was that big picture thinker. She always had answers to his questions.

"We will do both. Cake on her English calendar birthday and *Ayush homam* on her Hindu calendar birthday. Importantly, we will invite all her friends to both the celebrations." She said it simply, without a figment of thought in her mind about the expenses they were to incur for both. It was a small price to pay to soak and enjoy both traditional and modern living."

"There you go. I knew you will come up with a solution! I need to remember that the calendars are different. Hindu calendar 'star' birthdays don't necessarily fall on the same day every year. How can I forget that!" Ayush spoke. And he planted a gentle kiss on her forehead.

---

18   "The world is one family"

I Wish I Were White

She sank deeper into her sorrow – alone. Sunehari was stood up by her blind date. She had set it up on one of those *desi* dating apps. It was thirty minutes past their agreed time and the guy had left her waiting, the minutes stretching painfully. She ordered scotch on the rocks and gulped it down, looking at the bartender hoping at least he would figure out that she needed a refill. Quickly. The bartender had probably seen many such clients and knew what to do.

What the fuck is happening to me? Why am I am struggling to go on a date...? Her nemesis of a voice, the chatter in her mind was getting impatient. After the earlier debacle when the idiotic and cocky guy just told her he was not interested in her, her confidence has stooped low. So low that she was letting everyone walk over her. In all things.

Sunehari regularly scrolled through endless dating app profiles. A familiar wave of self-loathing washing over her. Every time a "*Desi* guy seeking..." popped up, her heart would snag on the unspoken preference – "for a fair girl."

I am not dark. Like those madrasis. But I must accept that I am fair like the dilliwalis. This went on all the time in her mind like a *mantra.* Unfortunately for her, playing this sad song so regularly in her mind had only cut those grooves much deeper and it had become a personality issue. Which was exacerbated by couple of mishaps in her dating life. But by *desi* standards, she was tall, fair, and stunning to look at. Physical attributes aside, which do make a good impression on the first dates, she was an engineer at a cool startup and earned well. But something was incomplete. She had a fault line to cross over. But she knew not what it was. One guy that she had liked very much, had the guts to spill the beans one day.

Sunehari imitated his words in her mind. *Mujhe gori ladki acche lagte hai.* But the bartender looked at her quizzically as to why she was shaking her head so vigorously. *Saala. Kya samajh rakha hai apne aap ko.* She was oblivious to the world outside. The *sruti* had taken her over. Her mind was just not ready from that scene she so often repeated mentally. And, *Gaalis* came naturally to her when she was upset.

Her friends did call her objectively light skinned for a North Indian, but Sunehari felt cursed by a shade that wasn't fair enough. Dates with non-*Desi* guys were awkward, a constant struggle to bridge cultural divides. She had grown up modern, with Western values and some of the creeps were looking to date an 'exotic babe'. Soon she gave up swiping right with other nationalities on the app. *She found her market fit, but the product was still not ready.* Her good friend, a marketing stud her told her the concept of product market fit. She hated it. Being objectified like a product. But it seemed true to her. And he was a good friend. Someone she can trust all times. And she did not hit him with a *chappal* that day of revelation.

She craved the comfort of shared traditions, the familiarity of *desi* humor. Bollywood. Song and dance sequences. Popcorn. *Paneer-tikka masala.* Talking in *Hinglish.* Sadly, the pond she was fishing in, the fish seemed to get attracted to the bait of "*gori*" girls, a term that scraped at her like sandpaper.

She was desperate. She imagined herself crying on the shoulders of the bartender. Like in the movies. But saner sense prevailed. She called him, settled the bill, and scooted soon after.

One evening, drowning her sorrows in YouTube makeup tutorials, a thumbnail caught her eye – "*Nirvana Shatakam: Who Am I?*" Curiosity piqued; Sunehri clicked. The speaker, a woman radiating serenity, was dissecting a human personality. It was logical, yet magical. She spoke of the eternal Self, the *Atman*, untouched by the limitations of the body, including skin color. Or the mind. Or its content. Nor was it the intellect. She spoke of pure consciousness, limitless and unchanging as a human's identity. The real person. She explained, with a logic that appealed to the nerdy brain of hers, what the real identity of a person was. As she listened, a spark ignited within Sunehri. Intellectually, it made perfect sense to her. But years of conditioning had built a wall between her intellect and her emotions. Importantly, skin color did not play any role at all.

The next day, Sunehri woke up with a newfound resolve. She deleted her dating apps. She seemed to have temporarily dropped the need for external validation of her worth. It was replaced by a quest for internal peace. An inquiry. She listened. And listened and some more of these lectures. Days became weeks and months. Driving became fun now, without traffic bothering her. She listened. She devoured books on Sanatana Dharma, the philosophy resonating deep within her. She started to cut through the grooves in her mind, turn off wrong switches in her intellect, push wrong conclusions and bad memories to cold storage and soon started connecting to the unchanging Self beneath the layers of insecurities.

Months turned to a year and half, and a quiet confidence bloomed within Sunehri. The way she carried herself changed, a newfound self-assuredness replacing the hunched shoulders of self-doubt. One day, while browsing a bookstore, a man bumped into her, his eyes widening in surprise.

"*Pardonnez!*" he exclaimed.

Sunehri smiled, brushing it off. "No worries, it happens."

They soon fell into conversation, discovering a shared passion for Indian philosophy. Pierre was a French architect who had visited Tiruvannamalai multiple times, drawn to the teachings of Ramana Maharshi. He spoke of his pilgrimage with reverence, a twinkle in his eyes that mirrored Sunehri's own awakening.

Their first date wasn't filled with awkward silences, but discussions about *karma, dharma,* and the quest for liberation. There was a comfortable understanding, a connection that transcended skin color or cultural divides. As they walked together under the twilight sky, Sunehri realized the *Nirvana Shatakam* had been more than just a lecture. It had been a key that unlocked the door to self-love, a love so profound it resonated with another soul across borders and backgrounds.

One day, Pierre gently slipped a ring into her hands. As he looked at her, both smiled. A smile of contentment and anticipation of shared life together.

The color of her skin, once a source of shame, became irrelevant. What mattered now was the golden light that shone from within. True to her name.

Bajji-Sojji Arranged Marriage

Memories of her youth unfolded as she found the letters hidden beneath her silk sarees. She had not touched that bundle of silk in ten years. Chicago became her home. Close to thirty years and life was…good.

Today, was her daughter's 16th birthday and next week she was going on a hike to Yosemite.

That is one of the many peaks I want to climb. After we moved here to US, I have not climbed and now my knees are weak. Thought Sarala and then relapsed into her time when she was her daughter's age.

The first time she trekked the Sahyadri's, she knew what her heart was missing. She wanted to be an explorer of new places. On foot. To climb every mountain peak of the world. It was time to close those books about the mountain ranges. She was ready to put her feet on earth. She was a firecracker of a woman, bursting with dreams of backpacking the globe. But the stunning landscapes, diverse flora, and fauna and importantly the rich cultural heritage of the mountain ranges narrowed her focus from backpacking to mountain climbing the peaks of the globe. *Someday, Everest….* she did think of it often though.

It was that high school trip that had changed her. She was part of the National Cadet Corps and their leader had organized a

Sahyadri trip. She more than liked that guy. The twenty odd highschoolers left for Pune from Mayiladuthurai in Tamil Nadu. In a train that chugged along at its own speed. Indian Railways had a nice charm in the early 70's and 80's. You did not know if the train you were boarding was yesterday's train or the correct one. The distance of approximately 1250 kilometers that should take about thirty hours took days sometime. But it was fun for the teens away from their parents.

She had a little something for him but did know how to label what it was. Her heart raced as he turned his head, a magnetic pull drawing her gaze. An accidental brush of his hand made her skin crawl, although in a nice way. Her legs felt weak when he spoke to her.

As they all trekked the mountains, preferring to go in the nighttime, to avoid the intense direct sun on them, Sarala suddenly twisted her ankle and was trodding along slowly behind the group. Somehow, she was left behind and got lost. Somehow. The others did not seem to have missed her. She was a quiet girl in any case. Quieter when he was around. In the darkness, she was all alone. She was not afraid, and her survival instincts had kicked in already. Adrenalin was high. The sharp trekkers knife in her hand to protect her from a slithering snake or a stray bat.

She saw a distant torch shine and walking towards her. She was thankful that someone was walking back. *They must have realized.* But she could not walk a step. The leg had swollen so much that if she poked the knife, it would probably ooze out all the blood from there. The light from the torch became dimmer and she noticed the sudden downpour. The water was camouflaging the light. She struggled to take out the raincoat from her backpack. And that's when it happened.

The cobra did not like an intruder. Sarala was sitting nearby the anthill that was below the tree she took shelter in. It hissed and two glinting diamonds for its eyes shone in the darkness. It was just a few moments from the time her hands were struggling to release the raincoat to the time she saw the snake. She froze. Her hands had gotten wound up in the plastic raincoat that she had bought. The knife was away from her hands. She closed her eyes for an instant, hoping it was all a dream and the snake would vanish when she opened her eyes again.

At that instant, she heard a loud sound and the cobra's dead head, severed from its slimy body lay next to her. It was him who arrived at the exact moment, like the Bollywood hero to save his love from distress.

She opened her eyes. She was shivering. It was cold, damp and she was drowned in a small wave of fear too. He hugged her tight, giving her the succor she needed. She melted in his hands. She kissed him. Passionately. He responded. Time just stood still for her.

They strutted together slowly, he occasionally carrying her or lending a hand. Progress was slow and steady, and they reached the group soon. But those few moments were the most beautiful moments of her life.

From that day onwards, they were a pair. Two years pass by since that fateful hiss and kiss, followed by many secret meetings. She knew she loved Raja. Raja was a passionate mountaineering guy. A year older to her and went off to college in the remote parts of Rajasthan. An occasional inland letter from him was all she got, that she hid from the prying eyes of her parents and her nosy sister.

Then one day, everything changed. Her dad came home with a heavy heart. "Raja fell from Hatu Peak in Shimla. His dad just told me that his body is coming here in two days." Their dads worked in the same insurance company. She did not know that though.

She ran into the backyard and was sobbing. Her first love was no more. Why hadn't the cobra taken her then? She grappled with the reality of a life devoid of him.

As she rummaged her secret suitcase, she read an old letter from him. And, he had said in that, *let us start an adventure tourism company and take people to all the mountain peaks of the world.* She had loved that idea.

As time went by, it healed some parts of her heart. She completed her BSc., and started working in a small firm. Listless work, but it kept her mind away from the parts that did not heal yet.

Then one day, her mom asked her to come home early. *Ponnu pakkarthuku varange inikki*[19]. She was to be paraded in front of someone. She knew not. And, if he liked her, she had no choice but to get married to him. Her parents believed in arranged marriages. Love, they scoffed, was a fleeting fancy,

---

19 Meaning, the prospective bridegroom & family are coming to 'see' you, the bride.

an unreliable compass for life. She had resisted the pressure to get married. But her mom was relentless and one day after a huge drama, she consented.

At 29, deemed "past her prime" by societal whispers, Sarala faced the prospect of marriage with a resigned sigh. Her mother, a master of emotional manipulation, played the "weak heart" card, while her father, the pragmatist, emphasized the lack of dowry and Meghashyam' s impressive salary (converted from dollars with a generous buffer, of course).

Sarala, yearning for freedom, attempted a final rebellion. "What if I eloped?" she'd asked, eyes pleading. But her parents' horrified reactions – her mother's tearful outburst, her father's stony silence – extinguished that spark.

Left with no choice, Sarala braced herself for a life with a stranger. She knew Raja was never going to come back. She picked the next best alternative and by evening, her life would have shifted gears.

The evening of the "bride viewing" arrived. Sarala, adorned in a silk saree and total lack of anticipation, served filter coffee and *bajjis* to Meghashyam and his entourage. Their eyes met – a spark she saw in his, a flicker of something more in his gaze. She cringed.

Then came the interrogation. Meghashyam's mother, the guardian of tradition, bombarded Sarala with questions – her culinary skills, her taste in television, her friend circle. It felt more like a job interview than a prelude to marriage. Yet, Sarala answered, hoping that her potential mother-in-law, if things worked out, would ask if she had any prior affairs. She knew that was a question no one would ask in such settings, but what's wrong in hoping!

Suddenly, the pivotal moment arrived. Meghashyam's mother turned to him, a knowing glint in her eyes. "Why don't you take her to a separate room and talk... in private?"

The room hushed. Sarala's heart skipped a beat as her mother's face broke into a radiant smile. In that simple request, a future unfolded. A closed door wasn't just privacy; it was a silent confirmation, a premonition – the marriage was *pukka*, a done deal. Horoscope matching, family referrals and all traditions, with all its weight and unspoken expectations, hinged on that single act. The boy and girl must like each other too. Compatibility was a check mark, but realism is important even in those villages. Especially if the girl is going abroad after marriage. For Sarala's mother, that closed door wasn't just the start of a conversation, it was the closing of a chapter and the beginning of a new one.

Sarala had hoped he would ask her atleast. About prior affairs. These America *mappillai* type are crazy lot – with a strong sense of ego and male superiority complex. But Meghashyam was already smitten by Sarala.

And he did not ask her any questions.

In two weeks, their marriage registered in the local municipality. A silent affair. A necessity to apply for her US visa.

Should I confide to Meghashyam now? She mused. Almost 30 years later!

Her open heart had healed completely and those painful stabs she had felt shooting from her heart all these years, somehow held no power. The first love was beautiful to remember, but life moved on.

A grateful silent prayer wishing Raja all happiness wherever he was – slowly murmured itself from her heart.

Aakir Naam Mein Kya Hai?

Meena waited in line for her coffee. The conference venue was crowded, with people moving in and out, and lines were longer than usual during breaks. She had even skipped a session to grab a coffee before her presentation, which was in an hour. Right now, her focus was on beating the headache with a much-needed cappuccino. But it was an unusually slow-moving line, and her patience was running thin. *What's the point of ordering ahead through an app if I still must wait?* she thought.

"Order 383, ready," the barista shouted. That was hers.

As she walked up to the counter, he asked, "Meenakshi Somasundaram?" His Chinese American accent tangled with the syllables, emphasizing the wrong parts. Meena disliked it when people buthered her name. To most, she was just "Meena" – short, simple, and easy. But, today, it seems the barista had glanced at her lanyard and decided to takle her full name.

"*Meena?* Yes. That's me." She grabbed her coffee, stingy with her smile.

Minutes later, the MC announced her name as the next speaker, the full, ceremonious "Meenakshi Somasundaram". *What were my parents thinking?* As the crowd clapped, she made her way onto the stage, mentally questioning if she really had to go through this torture every time. The presentation was an astounding success. And the demo went well too. As soon as she was off the stage, her thoughts swirled back to her name. *Super impractical. Who can even pronounce?*

She had relocated to the US five years ago. After doing her Masters, she took up a job at this cool startup. And this was the first major conference that she was a speaker in. It was an important one for their company. Few clients are likely to reach out.

"That was an awesome presentation Meenakshi," a gentle voice said from behind. It was James Scott, the CEO of one of their prospect companies. He too had fumbled her name.

Sensing that something was wrong, James asked. "Did I say your name right?"

She was embarrassed. She did not want to lie. Yet she did not want to offend him. She lied. "Thank you, James. Yes. It was fine. You can call me Meena for short."

James seemed curious. He was probably sixty. Or a little here and there. He was a widely traveled man. He apologized again. "I am sorry if I mispronounced your name. But I know very well that Indian names have meaning. What does your name mean?"

"Meenakshi refers to a goddess in the temple in a city called Madurai." She said.

"But there must be a meaning to that name." he insisted.

Can we talk shop? Why are you obsessed with my name? Call me X, Y or Z, let's move on and talk business.

She smiled at him sheepishly struggling to resolve the dichotomy of what was going on in her mind and what politeness and common sense demanded her to do.

But that comment stuck with her.

Later that evening she met Anjali for dinner. As they settled into their usual booth, Meena noticed a shift in Anjali's demeanor. Anjali, usually a whirlwind of chatter, was uncharacteristically quiet.

"What's wrong, Angie?" she asked, a slight concern lacing her voice.

Anjali had changed to Angie. They studied together and were thick friends.

"It's silly." Meena waited.

"I went out on a date last week with this amazing guy. He asked me what my name meant." Sam had asked Angie what Anjali meant.

"I did not know, and I did not care. I was Angie. Somehow that conversation put me off."

Now this was the rub she never needed. *Angie had completely changed. Name looks and behavior – all Westernized. But I could not let go of my roots. And stuck to shortening the name.*

Her curiosity was piqued. After Angie left, she Googled her own name, and her jaw dropped.

Meenakshi was a compound word of *Meena* and *Akshi*. "*Meena*" meant fish and "*Akshi*" meant eyes.

Her name had such a beautiful meaning, and she had shortened it. And butchered the meaning unknowingly.

Had I been asking everyone to call me fish for so long? How could I...?

A laugh escaped her. The irony was rich, but she felt an unexpected relief. It was time to embrace her name fully, even if it meant others struggled to pronounce it. *Desi* names weren't burdens—they were threads in the tapestry of unique identities, each carrying its own meaning, history, and spiritual significance.

School Mein Hindi Hi Kyon?

A wave of discontent rippled through the *desi* community in Fremont. The school board's decision to introduce Hindi as an elective ignited a firestorm of debate. WhatsApp groups buzzed with divisive messages; parents split along linguistic lines. Krishna, a Tamilian, scrolled through the messages, feeling a familiar unease.

"Hindi? What about Tamil?"

"Why not Telugu or Punjabi?"

"English is the common language, isn't it?"

"Do we even need this? What's the point?"

"Here, we can afford to forget our regional languages."

Krishna understood the frustration. Growing up in a fiercely Tamil household in Chennai, he was well-acquainted with the cultural clash surrounding the "Hindi imposition" narrative. As he read through the heated discussions, he thought back to his own experience learning Hindi. Dakshin Bharat Hindi Prachar Sabha, he recalled, was established over a century ago by Mahatma Gandhi. It was a movement born from the freedom struggle, with leaders believing a common language could strengthen national unity. His mother had insisted he and his sister learn Hindi—not only out of patriotism, but also because she believed in the intellectual benefits of multilingualism. His mother, a woman from a small village, had quickly mastered three languages. *"I think in Tamil, write in Kannada, speak in Telugu—and yes, even curse in Hindi!"* she would boast to their Nepali Gurkha guard.

"Krishna," she'd tell him, "words have meanings, but meanings must be understood in the right context. 'Duck' can mean a bird, or no runs scored in cricket. And if you translate everything from Tamil to English to understand it, you're missing something essential. To truly appreciate language, you have to think in it."

After school, Krishna was sent to the local "Hindi Mami" for extra classes. He progressed through Prathamik, Madhyamik, Rashtrabhasha, and so on until he protested in ninth grade, claiming he preferred cricket. His mother finally relented— but only somewhat.

It was his mom's small, persistent voice that echoed within him now – *wouldn't any Indian language be better than none?*

He pictured his daughter, Sweta, a second grader, immersed in American pop culture. Her knowledge of their heritage came mostly from occasional visits to the local temple. He longed for her to connect with her roots, to understand the stories that shaped their identity. She needed a tool—a language. At home, they spoke Tamil, but if she were to enjoy Meera's bhajans or appreciate her heritage deeply, Hindi might be the bridge.

Krishna knew English translations often fell short. Certain words, like *"arisi,"* could mean either uncooked or cooked rice—context mattered. Words like "*karma*," "*paapa*," and "*punya*" were easily misunderstood when translated as "work," "sin," and "good deed." And "*Bhagavan*" was not the same as "God" in the Abrahamic sense. In philosophy, terms like "*ahankara*," often translated as "ego," carried nuanced meanings related to self-identity and arrogance.

He wanted Anjali to grasp these subtleties and appreciate the richness of their heritage. Here in America, he believed clinging too tightly to regional identities was a luxury. For the future, he wanted his daughter to embrace a broader sense of Indian heritage.

The arguments for linguistic pride resonated with him. But here, in the melting pot of America, clinging to regional identities felt like a luxury they couldn't afford. The future generations, he believed, needed a broader understanding of their Indian heritage, a bridge that transcended linguistic borders. And, he had to agree with his *amma,* that some sort of formal vernacular learning is a must to appreciate a culture and civilization.

Krishna called his mother. She laughed. "*Muttal*[20]. I had trouble dragging you to *Hindi Mami* because you were in fifth grade, but Anjali is just in second. She won't resist like you did! Just enroll her."

Ignoring dissenting voices, Krishna signed Anjali up for Hindi classes, bracing for the inevitable questions: "Why Hindi and not Tamil?" But to his surprise, several parents—Malayalis, Kannadigas, Telugus, and Tamils—followed suit.

------

20   Idiot

As weeks turned into months, Anjali blossomed in her Hindi class. She'd come home humming Bollywood tunes, her eyes bright as she shared stories about Krishna and Rama in broken Hindi. Slowly, a bridge was being built—a bridge that connected her to a vibrant culture, one that transcended the boundaries of a single language.

One evening, Anjali proudly showed him her first written Hindi sentence: "*Namaste, Amma*," the note read. Krishna felt warmth wash over him. He knew the journey had just begun, but a seed had been sown—a seed of cultural awareness and unity that transcended linguistic differences. He had chosen connection over division, igniting a spark of heritage in his daughter's heart, a spark that no amount of regional politics could ever extinguish.

Cast(e) at Birth

What he was reading in *Drona Parva* of *Mahabharata* was especially contradictory.

Syam's thoughts went to the recent movie, *Kantara* that he saw. There is one scene when Shiva, the protagonist goes to the landlord's house. He just does not go inside the house. Neither the landlord invites him inside. The transaction was done outside, as the landlord regarded Shiva as unfit to be invited inside, believing he would defile his home. In another scene, the landlord asks his wife to sprinkle water all over the house to purify after Shiva forcibly enters the house. The landlord was considering himself superior and Shiva inferior, probably due to the differences in wealth. But Syam knew it was 'caste' based discrimination. That landlord's attitude was discrimination.

Higher caste people, looking down upon lower caste people, was the norm.

Syam squinted at the worn pages of the Mahabharata. He was rereading the pivotal scene where Drona, the revered teacher of the Pandavas and Kauravas, faced humiliation on the battlefield. As Drona, a *Brahmin* renowned for his archery skills, prepared to fight, his own student Bhima scoffed. "Why do you fight, Guru," they jeered, "is this the duty of a Brahmin?"

Syam frowned. *Drona, a Brahmin, facing ridicule for performing a warrior's duty? This wasn't right. Weren't Brahmins supposed to be the highest caste, the scholars, and priests? If they occupied the highest echelons of the caste pyramid that he so often saw, then they are not to be discriminated. Bhima was a kshatriya, a warrior. Lower caste than the brahmin. Then why the censure?*

He shut the book, a disquieting feeling settling in his stomach. Growing up, the concept of caste had always been associated with rigid hierarchy, with the "lower" castes being denied opportunities and facing discrimination. But here was a clear case of prejudice faced by a supposedly "upper" caste Brahmin.

He knew the society was built like what the movie depicted. Growing up, he also knew that some of his *brahmin* friends' mothers will not eat anything cooked in non-*brahmins'* home. And when the maid servant comes home to wash vessels, his mother's friend would rinse all of them again, or atleast sprinkle water on them to 'purify' them. Some of these *mami's* even referred to them as *sudras*. He found this strange and so did his friends. But they pushed that thought aside to go out and play. It was not something a nine – to eleven-year-old would spend their brainpower on, when the game of *gilli-danda* or *kabaddi* was more enticing. That attitude was clearly discrimination. But he did not know then.

He was shocked with this contrarian position being presented in Mahabharata. Reflecting on the rigid social structures depicted both in the film and his life, he starting reading.

As weeks slipped by, Syam devoured the *Bhagavad Gita*, finding himself engrossed by its verses and seeking answers.

Specifically looking for caste references in the book. There, he found no mention of castes. But the familiar four divisions were clearly there, referred by another *Sanskrit* word, *Varna*. As he read the meaning of the *sloka* in English[21], he realized that the four divisions that Lord Krishna talks about are based *not* on birth but by one's mental disposition /preferences (*guna*) and type of work one is inclined to do most effectively (*karma*). The wise and learned *Brahmins* conversant with the scriptures and ability to think clearly and unambigously[22], the courageous *Kshatriyas*, administrators and rulers maintaining the law and order in the state, the enterprising *Vaishyas* who knew how to handle money, trade, grow cattle, farming, and finally the service-oriented *sudras*, who did all kinds of work that was needed to be done in the society.

He knew where to get his answers.

'*Thathayya*[23], can you explain what the difference between *caste* and *Varna* is.' He asked in one of those regular phone calls. He was very close to his grandpa. A wise man, who was a retired diesel driver in the Indian Railways. Somehow in one of the trips, when his train was about to meet with a major accident, he had prayed to Swami Raghavendra of Mantralaya.

---

21   चातुर्वण्र्यं मया सृष्टं गुणकर्मविभागशः ।
तस्य कर्तारमपि मां विद्ध्यकर्तारमव्ययम् ॥ Gita 4.13 ॥
BG 4.13: The four categories of occupations were created by Me according to **people's qualities and activities**. Although I am the Creator of this system, know Me to be the Non-doer and Eternal.

22   Mahabharata Udyoga Parva *slokas 43.16, 43.20* describes in detail the definition of '*Brahmana*' as having twelve qualities and avoiding twelve types of faults. It :

23   Grandfather in Telugu

And the accident was miraculously averted. Forty years hence, he realized that there was some power beyond everything. He had delved to understand it. He met his spiritual *guru* who guided him through the wisdom of the scriptures. A transformed man, he was beginning to help other wayfarers in their spiritual path.

His grandfather chuckled, his eyes twinkling with wisdom. "The caste system, my boy, has been twisted and exploited over time. Originally, it was meant to be a flexible framework, ensuring social order and encouraging excellence in one's chosen field."

'Few thousand years ago,' He explained, 'people lived a life where professions were often passed down through families. That was because the societal structure was such that the next generation naturally learnt what they had to learn from the elders in the family – that is, the parents, grandparents and sometimes, even great, grandparents. Family was not a nuclear family, but very big joint families, with all uncles, aunts, cousins living under one roof and specializing in one major skill to earn their livelihood. A son of a farmer would naturally learn the skills of agriculture, while the son of a scholar would be drawn to learning. This wasn't discrimination, but a natural progression. Remember, it was those times of oral knowledge traditions. There were of course *gurukuls*, which was meant for anyone, irrespective of their caste to join and learn."

"Did many *sudras* join the *gurukul* in those days to learn?" asked Syam.

"You must think differently. We don't have any evidence of both answers to the question. Many may have. They may have not. But the different question you need to ask is – *were they stopped from formally learning?*" His grandfather paused.

Syam was waiting to hear more. He knew of one case – *Ekalavya*, who was stopped by Drona.

"*Satyakama Jabala* [24]was one such boy as an example. When he goes to sage Gautama, naturally he enquires about his parents. And he dutifully tells sage Gautama, what his mother told – *that she herself did not know who his dad was!*" He did not know his lineage. Neither did he say he belonged to one of the four *Varnas*. Still, he was accepted in Gautama's *gurukul* and he later becomes a famous sage." He spoke and added as if he understood what was going on in Syam's mind.

"*Ekalavya* story was different. We will discuss another day. But *Karna*, who was the son of a charioteer, was taught by *Parashurama, Drona,* and *Kripa.*"

Syam had to admit, "I did not know that." And he quickly asked, "Your logic that people picked up the profession of their family seems too vague to me. Not convinced."

Grandpa smiled and asked him a question, "Do you know where the last names of your friends, like Smith or Cooper, come from? Even in Europe, last names often tied back to professions, just as family vocations were historically embraced in India."

That was a big revelation for Syam. He had not understood this so far.

---

24   The sage's story is very popular in Chhandogya Upanishad.

"The true corruption," his grandfather continued, his voice grave, "came with the British Raj. They couldn't comprehend the concept of *Varna*. They wanted to figure out how to understand the Indian society of those times. They went around and asked people in different part of the country. They became increasingly confused when people said they did not know what their *caste* was. They just said that they do what their family had been doing for generations, to earn a living. The Brits saw the parallels from their own society, and they started dividing the country into *castes*, applying that word incorrectly to *Varna*. Their fundamental hypothesis, derived from their European way of life was that people doing a particular profession were born into a particular family. Obviously, they had assumed that *caste* was assigned at birth. Over time, this classification was used to exploit the society for their own benefit."

The British, Syam realized with a jolt, had deliberately solidified the caste system, labeling it as a rigid hierarchy with "higher" and "lower" castes. They even went a step further, creating a new fifth category – the *Dalits* – who were ostracized from society altogether. This fabricated system of "higher" and "lower" castes, fueled by colonial manipulation, had become the very definition of the caste system in modern India.

His grandpa was not done yet. He asked, "Can you ever write about a place that you never visited? Let alone talk about the culture and customs of the people living in that place?"

A puzzled look on Syam's face surfaced. *Where was he leading me to now?*

"If you ever get a chance to read a book called *The History of British India* by a Scotsman, James Mill you will know what I mean. He wrote that book in 1817, without even visiting India. How could he have ever been objective? Would we take it as a book of authentic history or a piece of fiction?" he asked, a minor irritation in his voice clearly visible.

"Over centuries, that book became one of the most quoted books to describe Indian society. It you google for it, you will know that it is praised by several quarters. Textbook publishers, subsequent researchers all reference this book in their works and derive authenticity. I can't understand the logic. It is like building a boat to ride in an oasis. The foundations of all the discourses we read today about caste, are nothing more than the figment of a misguided imagination."

Syam felt a wave of anger and disillusionment. The very fabric of his society, the foundation he thought he understood, was built on a foundation of misunderstanding and manipulation. But amidst the anger, there was a spark of hope. If the true intent of the *Varna* system was simple. It was an excellent observation by our ancient *rishis* of what the natural order of the universe is. Not everybody can be a strategist. Or an able administrator. Or a successful businessman. Or a service-oriented person. Each one of us have our own natural proclivities, inclinations, and affinity to a type of work, which in turn is based on the type of mind we have. And what would we say about the 'caste' of a software engineer who was an employee of a startup founded by his friend? And how would we classify the friend? Even if they both were siblings, we can safely say that the software engineer has more of a *sudra* characteristics, while the founder has more of *Vysya* characteristics. This is universally true. And the fluidity of people moving from one *Varna* to another is just the natural order of how their mind evolves.

But he was still tormented by what he saw in India even now. There are caste-based politics, reservation and so on. He voiced out his question.

"Unscrupulous elements will always take advantage of others. After the Brits left, protectionism continued. People realized that there was a new power that the caste division – the legacy of British provided them. They tried to take advantage of this, and unfortunately, it resulted in very rigid structures with no mobility between the different *Varnas*. The mobility was restricted by birth – these folks claimed wrongly but were highly successful to change the societal fabric completely." He noticed a tinge of sadness in his grandpa's voice.

"Sadly, the situation has worsened due to government policies. Reservation became a curse. Just because someone was born into 'forward caste', they were denied opportunities. Your dad, for example, did not get into medicine. He became a CA instead. While his good friend, Ramu, got into medicine based on the quota system for scheduled caste (SC). Both got the same marks in their college and your dad was just one rank above him in entrance exams. He is still your dad's good friend and they both do feel upset. Especially Ramu. He feels embarrassed that he got through not because of his merit but due to his caste. That's a big weight to carry for someone as talented and capable as Ramu. But they have made peace with the situation since long."

Syam knew Ramu uncle very well, but he did not know this backstory at all. All this was clearing the cobwebs in his mind.

And finally, what he heard from his grandpa shook him to the core.

"If anyone talks of *privileges* to upper castes, I recommend you ask them to read *Mahabharata*. The punishment is severely uneven. For the same crime, if the punishment is 1 unit for a person who is a *sudra*, it is twice for *vysya*, four times for *kshatriya* and eight times for a *Brahmana*."

With newfound determination, Syam decided to educate himself and others. He started a blog, dissecting ancient texts and sharing the true meaning of *Varna*. He spoke at community gatherings, challenging misconceptions and urging people to focus on fulfilling their *dharma*, their inherent duty, irrespective of their birth. He encouraged people to take stock of their proclivities and interests that come naturally to them and then follow the profession that closely matches those. The path wouldn't be easy, but Syam knew it was necessary. He had to help dismantle the system of oppression that had festered for centuries, and rebuild a society based on the true principles of his ancestors – a society that valued duty, not birth.

Close to the heels of SB403 being vetoed by Californian governor, one day he was invited by one of the major podcasters for a debate on caste system. And he so looked forward to beating the proponents of SB403 with logic. He knew his facts better now.

ROI of Guilt

Chandra sat in his sleek office, surrounded by glass walls that overlooked the bustling city below. His desk was a symphony of screens, each displaying a different aspect of his work: emails, stock prices, project updates. He was a senior executive at a tech giant, a man who thrived on productivity, efficiency, and the relentless pursuit of success.

His phone buzzed, interrupting his rhythm. It was his weekly reminder: "Call *Amma*." *Amma*—his mother, the anchor of his life. She lived in a small village in India, her days filled with simple routines. Every Friday, she waited for his call, her eyes lighting up when his name flashed on her ancient Nokia phone.

Chandra dialed her number, leaning back in his ergonomic chair. The connection crackled to life, and he heard her voice—a blend of love, warmth, and a hint of mischief. She rattled off the mundane details of her week: the lentil curry she cooked, the neighbor who visited, the *puja* she performed. Her TV serials, with their convoluted plots and dramatic twists, were her lifeline.

He listened half-heartedly, toggling between screens. "Hmm," he murmured, feigning interest. His mind raced ahead, calculating profits, deadlines, and market trends. His mother deserved more, but he was a master multitasker. He could juggle conference calls, board meetings, and family obligations without missing a beat.

Suddenly, he dropped everything he was doing to hear his mother say, "Maybe we should talk some other time, Chandra. Looks like you are busy."

Guilt gnawed at him. He remembered another time—a distant memory that tugged at his conscience. When he was a child, bedridden with chicken pox, *Amma* had abandoned her work at the Indian Space Research Organization (ISRO). She was a brilliant scientist, a woman who had helped launch satellites into orbit. But none of that mattered when he lay feverish and itchy. She had named him Chandra after the moon, the goal ISRO was driving for. To get to the moon, at less than the budget of a mega starrer, mega budget movie.

She had sat by his side, reading stories, wiping his forehead, and singing lullabies. Her eyes had held a universe of love, and he had felt cocooned in her presence. The satellite launches, the equations, the critical missions—they all had faded into insignificance for her. She had chosen him over her career, her passion, her dreams.

Chandra's mind voice whispered, *What have I become? A man who values spreadsheets over conversations, profits over connections.* He remembered the day he left for the United States, chasing ambition and opportunity. *Amma* had stood at the airport, tears streaming down her face. She didn't understand why he had to go, but she had kissed his forehead and whispered, "Make us proud, my son."

And he had. He climbed the corporate ladder, amassed wealth, and built an empire of zeros and ones. But at what cost? His heart ached as he imagined *Amma's* wrinkled face, waiting by the phone, her world reduced to a weekly call.

"No *Amma*, I just got interrupted by something." He lied. Blatantly.

That evening, he sat across from his wife, Meera. He hesitated, then spilled his guilt-laden thoughts. Meera listened, her touch grounding him. "Go," she said. "Book a flight to India. Be with your mother. She's not asking for the moon."

She stirred *chai*, her eyes knowing. "Chandra," she said gently, "you're chasing shadows. Success means nothing without the people who love you."

And so, Chandra boarded the next flight. The city lights faded, replaced by star-studded skies. The scene outside looked the same from all windows, and he recalled the first flight when he was in economy class and was so excited by the beauty of the plane taking off leaving behind the city. Business class windows don't have any extra privileges. He knew that well.

As the plane touched down, he felt the weight of his choices—the missed birthdays, the absent anniversaries, the silent Sundays. He had become busy the past few years, after having sold his startup. And he was a workaholic. Focused on goals and success. Money defined his life. More the merrier.

For the first time, he felt exposed. Caught by emotions that did not play any part in his cold, calculating world.

Amma stood very surprised as she opened the door at 3AM in the morning. She didn't ask why he had come; she simply hugged him, and she wept.

"I am here for just two days *Amma*. Felt like meeting you." He spoke.

They sat on her porch, sipping *chai*, talking about nothing and everything. The TV serials played in the background, their absurdity now endearing. He switched off all gadgets and drove her everywhere. To the few nearby temples, she could not go since her accident in the bathroom a year ago. After dad passed away, she had became lonely and the accident curbed her mobility, making her a prisoner in her own home. She stopped serving the *Sai Satsangs* that she was part of all her life.

Seeing Chandra in white *dhoti* and *kurta*, her mom gave an approving smile.

"Yes *Amma*. I dress up for the occasion. This is what is appropriate for the temple visit, isn't it? You surely don't expect me to come in my business suit to a temple. But I will indeed be in my favorite Armani when I go for my meetings." He spoke.

And off they went to the nearby Tirupathi Balajee temple.

Chandra realized that time wasn't money; it was life. And life was in these moments—shared laughter, quiet conversations, and the warmth of a mother's touch. He vowed to be present, to listen without distraction, to cherish the mundane.

As the sun dipped below the horizon, *Amma* asked, "Why the sudden trip?" He did not respond.

Two days later he was on his way back. He was preparing for an important client meeting and had to get into the mood. Couple of shots down, the snakes in his mind sprang up to take charge. He was adapting to the culture of the place he was flying to. He did not realize but it was as if he took off a hat and wore another one. The hat of love towards his mom, guilt and shame towards his own attitude replaced with a pure capitalist version. Not only the place where he was going to was telling him what he should be wearing and which specific suit from his wardrobe would give him a power look, it even seemed to influence his thoughts.

"How much this two-day trip really cost me? I can peg a dollar number to it. Apart from the last-minute expensive flight tickets, I also was doing nothing at all. It all adds up." He asked himself and his mind began evaluating the cost & ROI.

ROI of guilt.

Far behind the aisles, he could hear the small baby cry. And he felt irritated.

Underwear

Ten years. It had been that long since Rahul and Pavan had last slapped mosquitoes on a Chennai rooftop, dreaming of adventures beyond their bustling city. Now, their reunion unfolded in a noisy New York diner, a stark contrast to their childhood haunts.

Rahul, still sporting a familiar mop of unruly hair, grinned at Pavan. "Look at you, Mr. American Hotshot! You barely speak Tamil anymore."

Pavan chuckled, a hint of self-consciousness in his laugh. "Come on, Rahul, it's been five years. Gotta get assimilated, right?" He was all crisp chinos and a neatly trimmed beard, a far cry from the *kurta*-clad boy Rahul remembered.

"Assimilate? You mean Americanize yourself?" Rahul teased.

Pavan shrugged, taking a bite of his burger. "Maybe. It's a different world here, Rahul. Here, it's all about the hustle."

Rahul's brow furrowed. "The hustle? But Pavan, what about all those temple visits, learning chanting and *slokas*? Didn't that matter?"

It did not miss that Pavan was constantly checking his mails and responding to texts, half attentive to the conversation. Rahul was visiting the US on a rare business trip, and they decided to meet. Ever since he left India, Pavan had not come back home, even once. He always was concerned about his visa status and how his travel to India would impact his green card. And Pavan had taken up teaching in a government school. It was through his school that he was here on a week-long seminar to learn about different pedagogical methods.

Pavan and Rahul attended the same school, same extra classes. Their parents were thick friends and if you found one, the other was bound to be there somewhere around within a few yards. Never more than the cricket ground distance.

Pavan snorted, a humorless sound. "Those things are great for inner peace, maybe. But here, inner peace won't get you a promotion or a fancy apartment. Here," he tapped his chest, "ambition is king."

He paused, a mischievous glint in his eyes. "Speaking of ambition, do you know when I truly became Americanized?"

Rahul, intrigued, leaned closer. "When?"

Pavan grinned. "Underwear. It all started with underwear. For five years, I clung to my VIP Frenchies, the most comfortable things ever invented, mind you. But then, one day, my friend dared me to try Calvin Kleins."

Rahul burst out laughing. "Seriously? Underwear is your turning point?"

Pavan held up a hand. "Don't underestimate the power of good underwear, Rahul. Those Kleins felt…different. Powerful, even. And that's when it hit me. Back home, contentment was a virtue. Here, it's the enemy. You gotta be hungry, gotta strive for more."

A pang of sadness flickered in Rahul's chest. He saw a truth in Pavan's words, the relentless pursuit of success that defined America. But something felt off. Pavan seemed to sound like Duryodhana in *Mahabharata*. Duryodhana was ambitious, had an insatiable hunger for power. He had argued with his dad that *being contented is being an enemy of wealth and power.* Insinuating that the goal of life was wealth and power. Deluded by the means and end. He did not ask in those times – for what purpose should I gain wealth and power. And like Mr. D in *Mahabharata*, his good friend seemed to have flipped the means for goals. Contentment, Rahul believed, wasn't the opposite of ambition; it was the cherry on top, the quiet satisfaction that came after achieving your goals.

He looked at Pavan, his friend transformed into a stranger. "Maybe, Pavan," he said gently, "maybe the goal here isn't just the hustle. Maybe it's finding a balance, a way to be ambitious while holding onto the things that truly matter."

Pavan looked away, a flicker of doubt crossing his face. Perhaps, in the blinding lights of ambition, he'd deliberately forgotten the warmth of a temple chant, the comfort of his mother tongue. The reunion had rekindled a part of himself he'd buried deep, a part that yearned for something more than just the next promotion, the next big purchase.

The conversation drifted to other topics, but Rahul knew a seed had been sown. Maybe, just maybe, Pavan, the American Hotshot, would one day rediscover the value of inner peace and inner contentment.

Belle from Baburvani

She was livid.

The fairy lights strung across her studio San Francisco apartment cast a harsh glow on her today. As if it was reflecting the simmering anger in her. Maya was not happy. The India she had grown up was truly secular; much more than the US she thought; but in the last ten years, as she tracked the country's progress, her objectivity was being put to test.

The temple. It was a *kebab mein haddi* for her.

How can a government openly support construction of a temple? Isn't that in direct violation of the constitutional principles that the founding fathers of India set soon after Independence in 1947?

Her childhood memories flashed through her. The pride with which she celebrated Independence Day, Republic Day, Gandhi Jayanthi, Children's Day and of course festivals. *We had no school those days and it was fun to play kho-kho and other games with the girls. Sometimes, even sneak out with the boys for gol-gappe.* While her dad was not happy that they were celebrating festivals when the kids had to be at school and everyone was productive doing some work or the other, Maya was mightily pleased to get an extra holiday!

Maya had grown up in the late seventies and eighties in a small place nearby Kolkata. Baburvani, Jangalmahal about 200 kilometers from the hustle and bustle of the city. Without the sounds of creaking trams. Bullock cart was the main transport for the villagers with the occasional bus service that was known for its petulance. Always doing what it wanted to do, without any adherence to the timetable.

She was happy to move to US for her grad school and had not looked back. Single, living a very simple life, she was focused on investing her money in social causes in *desh*. Nearing sixty – a milestone, she had wished the world were not as polarized as it was.

Ram temple in *Babri masjid* site was not needed. That bothered her. She mused that she indeed had her dad's genes.

Her dad was a fierce communist. His life vaguely resembled to that of Ishwar Chakraborty (minus the dramatization that was presented) in the 1965 movie, *Subarnarekha*, titled after the *gold-streaked river* that ran nearby their village. Her dad had faced immense hardships after his parents sought refuge in India due to the partition. Then the Hindu-Muslim riots followed. Finally, the Marxist, Naxalite ideologies influenced his thinking. He had become an atheist. Strange that he grew up in Baburvani, a name the village must have picked up from the Sikh literature that talks about Babur's invasions.

Her dad had strongly objected to her going to the temples. She was born in a Hindu family, but her dad's ideals had influenced her so much. The Jhargham Rameswar temple was supposed to have been built by Lord Rama himself, but he never allowed her to go visit. But he had not known that she had bunked school to go there with friends.

With malice towards one and all wrote Khushwant Singh. She argued. That's the same as *with love towards one and all.* Being equal towards all faiths – by practicing none was her way of respecting all religions.

She was truly upset. She had to talk to somebody. Who better than her school friend Meenakshi who had become an authority on Indic studies. She picked up the phone.

"I don't think we are going in the right direction. This act is not secular."

Meenakshi challenged her. Wizened by not only age, but also extensive research and study about Indian civilization and culture, she asked, "Secularism is a Western concept created out of the Westphalian treaty in the 17th century. Its main motive was to bring an end to the Christian denominational wars between the Protestants and Catholics. The idea of nation-state was created to divest the political power of Roman Catholic church. It is a force-fit of an ideology that does not work."

"So, what is the alternative? Especially in India? Are you saying India should become religious country? Our founding fathers ensured that we were 'secular' when drafting the constitution…."

Meenakshi did not let her complete her sentence. She threw up a lesser-known fact at her.

"It was during the dark days of free India that Indira Gandhi introduced the 42nd Constitutional Amendment Act of 1976 that inserted the word, 'secular' to the Constitution."

Maya's jaw dropped. She let Meenakshi continue.

"When the princely states came together to form the modern India, the erstwhile rulers negotiated with India to ensure that the culture of their kingdoms and their way of life was protected. That is why the name of the country is *India, that is Bharat* – accepting the way of *Bharatiyata.*"

"Actually, in the West, secularism often means keeping religion out of public life. But in ancient Bharat, it was always about inclusion. The kings facilitated all religions, built facilities for everyone, and ensured everyone felt respected. Look at Emperor Ashoka, who patronized all religions – Buddhism, Jainism for example. He did not have to struggle though because fundamentally, in *Sanatana Dharma* there are so many different, contradictory points of view[25]. Including the POV of an atheist. All were accepted. It was not easy though in practice for future kings, but they strived to deliver *dharma*. The civilization was predominantly built on the fabric of *dharma* which are nothing but principles of natural justice. There was no force fitting of anything. Different kingdoms, different rules, yet all united by *dharma.*"

"Can you elaborate? You are using words like *dharma* and natural justice that may have different meanings to me?"

---

25   Called *darshana*

"*Dharma* is a complex topic. We will keep it for another day. But I just want to say that it was codified in our several scriptures as to how an individual should live their life, how they should relate to others in family, in the society etc. Moreover, there were code of conduct for rulers and administrators as well as methods of punishment etc. All these were the foundation of our Constitution, and this foundation was based on a system of justice that was equitable and just to everyone."

"This whole concept of religious fights in current India..." Maya mumbled. "It just doesn't sit right with me."

And she slowly slipped in the real question to her friend.

"Why should the government support construction of Ram Temple in Ayodhya? Can't they have left the *Babri Masjid* as it is?"

An exasperation sounded in Meenakshi's voice. Her friend who was seeing India and the conflict through the eyes of the media she was consuming did not know the facts. But she answered her in another way. She did not want to argue the facts with her. Her job was to help her friend change her wrong perspective.

"Remember as children we went to the Rameswar temple in Jhargham?"

How can she forget that? That was so beautiful. And must be protected from damage. It was a world heritage site with an immense history to it. She had been sending money regularly to support such unique heritage sites in India.

"If you were to lose that one day to the floods of *Subarnarekha*, how would you feel?" Meenakshi asked.

"It would be terrible. That has memories of our childhood. It is art and can't be lost. It is history – even if I don't believe that Rama built it…."

"Would you make attempts to reclaim that site or not?" Meenakshi asked Maya. She carefully avoided the word *temple* and instead called it a *site*. She knew Maya still espoused her dad's fierce communist and atheist views of life.

"Absolutely. I will wait for an appropriate time for the floods to subside and then perhaps petition to build a dam that would divert the waters." Maya was very clear. She needed that piece of history, of her childhood to be there for the posterity to learn and enjoy.

"So, what's wrong reclaiming what is due to Hindus on which the mosque was built?" Meenakshi's voice hit her heart hard.

The little girl from Baburvani in her understood the damage that was inflicted by foreign invasions and attacks on *Bharatiyata* culture. The temples were the heart of culture. But the invaders not so kind. They inflicted damage on people, imposed hard punishments, collected high taxes. Yet, the followers persisted. They protected their culture and the visible symbols of culture – the temples. She recalled the different themes each of the temples had been to. Dance, music, art, stories, ethics, and even passionate sexual sculptures in temples. All were OK. She knew it. That was her culture. It had survived for thousands of years of onslaughts from the North.

If it had indeed survived, then why should we not be proactive to protect and preserve?

The silence on both ends of the phone said more than the words the friends spoke for an hour.

Cosmic Dance

Neeti swiped right and her blind date was set with Ram. He seemed good. She had carefully perused several profiles on the app to make sure that she was not going out with weirdos who get serious. She hated it. She was ready for a new adventure. Picked up the nice red dress that she had bought for this new date.

The last boyfriend was getting too serious. He was beginning to talk crazy ideas like *marriage, children vagairah vagairah.*

Neeti clutched her latte, the frothy swirl mirroring the agitation in her stomach.

Children. The mere thought brought forth a mental image of sleepless nights, sticky fingers, and a career trajectory nosediving faster than a rogue rocket.

She was doing great professionally. She was a fast climber too. At thirty, she had become the director of investor relations at a major company. And, with her passion for environment, conservation she had become an active advocate of the mute, all bearing, ever giving, kind, nurturing Mother Earth. She had traced the root cause of the rapid rise in carbon dioxide in the air and the consequent global warming to more people on earth. She accepted the climate science and knew distinctly that more people on the planet only meant more resources.

"In *Umreeka*," as she lovingly referred to America, in some gibberish language that only she and her close friends subscribed to, "we can truly follow our passions. Without any inhibitions. If we are within the bounds of law." She stated her position quite often.

She had left India for the shores of Boston to do her Masters. Seven years after, she had adapted to the American way of life as easily as a fish to water. She hailed from a small village in MP – Khargone. Located on the bank of the Kunda river the city was known for many things – cotton and chilly amongst them being the foremost. But little-known facts about her town was that it was also the home to beautiful temples, forts, and tombs. The influence of both Hinduism and Muslims was very visible. And so were the frequent violent communal eruptions.

There were a lot of restrictions growing up. Parents had been careful not to let her stay late in the evening. They enforced her to dress modestly. They had been wary of her friendship with boys. They never liked it, and took every opportunity to chide her on her friends.

If you want to restrict me so much, why did you even give birth to me? She had lamented and cried quite often in the kitchen, her mother silently doing the *rotis*, half-listening to her cries. *Am I such a crazy kid or do you think that children are stupid? I was the result of your need to have sex.*

Here, she was free to do what she wanted. The pendulum had swung the other way. She had best of both worlds. Money, freedom to spend, time to enjoy hikes, parties with friends and the whole nine yards that America offered. She came as a student, became an economic migrant and soon the place grew on her. The memories of Khargone started to fade quickly. With every new swipe on the Tinder app, she made new acquaintances. She slept with a few too. No strings attached. No qualms. She was never concerned about getting pregnant. She had taken all the precautions she could take – pills, IUDs et.al and still insisted on a condom in all her rencontres. Motherhood, she believed, was a societal construct, pressure points for women, not an instinct. And she was clear – yes to sex, no to baby making. Sex was a biological need. That's it.

And she found a way of arguing her logic out with friends.

"I just don't get it," she declared to her friend Priya, "Why are kids seen as this ultimate life goal? They're expensive, messy, and are a massive environmental footprint. Motherhood is overrated. I will not do it. And on top of it, we are already close to 9 billion people. There aren't enough resources to support new entrants to this planet earth. Having children is not environmentally wise decision."

Priya chuckled, a knowing glint in her eyes. "The eco-warrior stance? Classic Neeti."

The pub was lively. She had always liked the DJ there. Relaxing with a beer and an occasional reef was her standard practice. She had never cared to impress the guys she dated. She just did what she wanted to. And let things evolve organically.

The instant she saw Ram, she was attracted to him. There was something about him that she could not place her finger on. But surely, he had a presence. He was an anti-thesis of her. A teetotaler, who picked up a virgin Mary and water without ice. But she did not think he was a loser. Something interested her.

They seemed to hit it off well. The first date was uneventful. Each basically sharing a bit about what they did. But some of what they talked struck with her.

"I do organic farming and live in the ranch outside the city." Said Ram.

Till then, she had not realized that she was speaking to the owner of Ram Organics, one of the well-known small brands in the town. She particularly was tracking this company because of the kind of sustainable work what they were doing. His company came across as honest, simple and made it easy for consumers to buy organic food that was not too expensive compared to Whole Foods. Better taste too. She had occasionally ordered from them and was always surprised with their consistency.

"I did not know that my date would be you." She blushed a bit.

Few more dates later, they seem to have struck an easy-going relationship. They moved from the 'strangers and acquaintances' zone to something beyond. Not a 'lover's' zone but perhaps into the 'good friends' zone. She found him intelligent, funny, and held a profound view of life that challenged her own.

For the first time Neeti wanted this to work. She cared. But she did not know why. At times, she did have her doubts if Ram was a con man. *If he was, what was he trying to swindle from me? I would have gladly let him sweep me off my feet to land either in his bed or mine.*

He never spoke about marriage or children. Perhaps he wanted things to evolve too.

And she was mentally preparing for the eventual question. *If he did propose, would I say yes to marriage but strictly no kids. Or should I convince him that we should live-in together with no strings attached?* She was a seesaw of emotions. Swinging wildly from one end of the spectrum to the other. Somedays wanting to live the life that she imagined Ram would want to have with her. Some other days, so adamant that her bohemian rhapsody continue all through her life.

He asked that crucial question that changed the trajectory of her thinking.

"What is your ultimate goal in life?"

"To be successful." She spoke.

"How?"

That's when she realized that she was comparing herself with an ideal role model and was aspiring to reach that ideal step by step. A promotion, a pay hike or a new car took her one step in that direction. And that's how she had defined success.

One part of her thought it was a trick question. She was smart enough to turn around the question.

"It's your turn. To answer." She smiled. Relieved that she can judge him now.

It was his answer that resonated with her the entire week that made her want to talk with him again.

He had said, "I see a grand happening in this entire universe. Everyone playing a part. Every living being and non-living being. As if there was grand master orchestration going on. I want to be part of that cosmic dance."

She looked surprised. Was taken aback. She asked him to explain.

"As a farmer, I see a reality in front of me. Seeds to plants to trees. Then flowers and fruits. Then seeds from fruits and the cycle continues. Not to forget the shade to the wayfarers. Or honey to the bees. Or a home to the earthworms in their roots. Or to the various other living beings, especially we humans who enjoy the produce from these trees. The soil, water, sunlight, air all serving the seed and in turn transforming it to grow and contribute. "

She had never thought of this. But it was a fact. She could not refute it. But she wore a curious look on her face, and he continued.

"Is the tree a success. Surely yes. It grew. It served. And it continued in another form of the tree, from the seeds from its fruit. The tree had its own limitations. Can't walk. Or talk. Maybe think or maybe not. But one thing for sure. Even with all its limitations, it was a success. Just doing its part in the cosmic dance."

She agreed.

"As I think deeper into this, it seems to me that this dance at a cosmic scale has been happening in many ways. Like the tree example, think of the soil. It contributed to the tree, which in turn contributed to the welfare of the others."

She had read somewhere, and she blurted it out, "Of course, what we eat – veggies or non-veggies is just a conversion of earth, water, sun, air and space."

"And it may seem like a coincidence. Chance encounters that we may dismiss as random. But is it random at all? If you zoom out, the earth being in its orbit is part of the cosmic dance. The earth being at the right distance from the sun so that life can happen here and nowhere else, is a part too." Then he went silent.

She wondered for what it seemed like really a long time.

"I am trying to figure out my role in this cosmic dance." He said and looked at her, as if asking her if she wants to dance with him.

"What you say is very interesting. Let us play this Q&A game for some time more and figure out the possibilities together." She volunteered to be the guinea pig in this thought experiment.

"Are we giving each other permission to ask difficult and uncomfortable questions?" he asked.

She nodded yes. The game was interesting, and she knew that he was going to lead her into the dance.

"What we need to figure out first is, if the status quo of our lives is already a part of this cosmic dance or not." He spoke.

"I think it is. Else, we will not be alive. I am doing my job, earning and contributing to the society by paying taxes.

My tax dollars help in building the infrastructure, pay for social security, defense….and I spend money to buy. Which in turn helps companies to produce goods, who in turn offer employment and those employees in turn take care of themselves and their families." She said it all in one breath. Proud that she was indeed dancing. Absolutely logical answer to the question.

"Ya. I too feel the same way. But I don't think it is sufficient. What do you think differentiates our dance with the dance of the tree?"

"I don't think they are different." She spoke. Quickly she corrected herself.

"It is a bit different in the sense that the tree does the dance it knows to do, only in the service of others. All the seed does is to grow. Which is its true nature. And in the process, it is serving everybody else. All through its life. And in many ways."

He loved her answer. He built on top of it.

"With fewer resources than what we have. We can talk, walk. We have free will and ability to choose. With these additional resources, how else can we be better?" he spoke.

She did not realize that she had already gone too deep into this mind game. There was a part of her that was asking her to backtrack and get away from this game. But it was too late.

"Honestly, I think the difference is that we work for ourselves first and when we have 'extra' left over from our wants & needs, we contribute to others welfare. Or we are forced to part a bit of our work compensation in the form of tax. Who doesn't want lower taxes? Or no taxes?" she said.

He again built on top of her response. Nodding in violent agreement with her.

"I think you are saying that our approach is wrong. I agree. If we were to completely change our approach, what should we be doing differently starting today?"

She spoke, "I think we would change our mindset first. Speaking of myself, I will not go to work to earn a salary anymore. I will go to work to solve the problem that I am passionate about – environment. Protecting our environment for inter-generational use will become my responsibility. But today, earning my pay is my primary responsibility. When that shift happens in my mind, the pay would be transactional. I will be then dancing in the tango knowing the steps quite well."

Ram said, "Take this thought exercise to an extreme." And he continued, "What is that we can do that is completely selfless? And it also resembles what the tree does, generations after generations?"

She knew the answer. But did not want to say it.

Then he slowly asked her. "Why do you not want to have children?" A simple straightforward question. Out of the blue.

"Are you proposing?" she asked. They had enough comfort with each other to have this conversation.

"Not yet. Maybe not. Maybe yes." Mysterious for the first time.

She spoke. This time with utter honesty. "I will have to reconsider what I thought about children so far. I was happy the way my life was. But not anymore after this conversation."

Ram then said, "If ever you want to repay the debt to your ancestors for having created that seed that you were, and now beginning to blossom into a tree to serve others, I would love to tango with you. "And slowly pushed his chair back and went down on his knees. A spotless diamond ring in his right hand and looked up to her in anticipation.

Neeti pondered his words. The focus wasn't on personal desires, but on a cosmic responsibility. Maybe children weren't just a burden, but a continuation of the grand happening, a link in the chain of existence. She had questions. The environmental concern still lingered, but Ram's perspective had ignited a new spark within her. Perhaps, she thought, with conscious parenting, with teaching her children the importance of environmentalism, they could contribute not just to the cycle of life, but to its sustainability. Or maybe what value is protecting the environment itself is, if the 'inter-generation' does not even materialize?

She did not take the ring then.

Months later, Neeti sat beside Ram, a hand resting on her baby bump, a soft smile gracing her lips. They just finished a Zoom call with Neeti's parents, and she had broken down, apologizing to her mom for the harsh, insensitive words she had once spoken in her kitchen. Her mom had forgotten, but Neeti had not.

The grand cosmic dance had taken hold, and she was ready to waltz with it. Motherhood, once a distant thought, was now an exciting step in the eternal rhythm of existence.

5 Pillars, 10 Commandments & Dharma

M s. Patel stood before her high school world religions class, feeling like a tightrope walker about to step onto a wire strung between skyscrapers. She had navigated the clear waters of explaining Islam and Christianity easily, but now she faced the vast, swirling ocean that was Sanatana Dharma. And it bothered her that it was her own, that was so confusing to understand and importantly to explain to others. Her only excuse was that she was an atheist, or at best an agnostic, who cared less about any religion, including her own. But she had a job to do, and she took that job seriously. However a thought did cross her mind – *how come I am able to grasp the concepts of the other two religions, but not Hinduism?*

In her class, she was only tasked to educate the kids on the basic beliefs of these three religions. At the level she was teaching, she obviously had to simplify the concepts to present a contrast between the three major religions. It was not a class to preach but teach and let the children explore the ideas by themselves.

"Alright, class," she began, her voice a steady beacon in the sea of curious faces before her. "We've explored Islam and Christianity. We've examined their core tenets & beliefs Now, we're about to embark on a journey through Sanatana Dharma, often referred to as Hinduism."

She paused, searching for the right words, feeling like an artist with a blank canvas and a palette of infinite colors. How could she paint a picture of something so vast and intricate?

"In our previous lessons, we explored the tenets of Holy Trinity in Christianity. We understood the concept of God in Islam, known as Allah. We talked of the Bible, Holy Koran and the ten commandments, chiseled in stone like immovable mountains as well as five pillars, those sturdy columns supporting the faith. "

The class had liked her metaphors of pillars and stone carvings. Something that would etch in their memory, especially useful to answer the questions in their exam. A chuckle rippled through the class, as she mentioned these metaphors again as a way of recapping the last class.

"But *Sanatana Dharma*," Ms. Patel continued, "well, it's more like trying to capture a cloud in a jar. It's there, it's real, but it shifts and changes, taking on new forms as you observe it. "

"You would be surprised that there is no word in *Sanskrit*, the language of this tradition, called *Hindu*. It was a name of Persian origin that was assigned to these followers." She chose to give out a useful nugget of information that they will remember. Especially if it has a surprise element.

As the students murmured to each other realizing the gravity of what she said, she wrote *'dharma'* on the board, the chalk scratching out the word that was both simple and infinitely complex.

"This concept, *dharma,* is at the heart of Sanatana Dharma. But unlike the heart in your chest, with its steady, predictable rhythm, *dharma* is more like the rhythm of life itself – sometimes steady, sometimes chaotic, always adapting."

A student raised her hand, her brow furrowed in concentration. "What exactly does *dharma* mean, Ms. Patel?" She surely was not impressed with her continued use of metaphors and analogies. She was annoyed it was quite confusing.

"Excellent question, Sarah. *Dharma* often translated as 'duty' or 'righteousness', but those are just facets of its true meaning. Like the light through the prism, *dharma* splits into many colors – it's about living in harmony with the cosmic order, fulfilling one's purpose, and doing what's right based on one's role and circumstances."

Ms. Patel could see the wheels turning in her students' minds, some spinning smoothly, others grinding against this new, complex idea. The same was true of her too. She was learning herself. Or like her engineer boyfriend would say, *changing the engine mid-flight.*

"Unlike the other religions we've studied, Sanatana Dharma doesn't have a fixed set of rules that apply to everyone. Instead, it offers guidelines that can change based on a person's age, occupation, and life stage. It's less like a map with a clear 'X marks the spot', and more like a compass, pointing you in the right direction but leaving the journey up to you."

"But how do people know what to do?" Alex asked, his voice tinged with frustration. "It sounds so... vague."

Ms. Patel nodded, acknowledging the difficulty. "It can seem that way, Alex. In *Sanatana Dharma*, individuals are encouraged to use their judgment and conscience. They're guided by ancient texts, teachers, and traditions, but ultimately, they must decide what *dharma* means for them in each situation. It's like being given a musical instrument without sheet music – you have the tools, but you must learn to create the melody yourself."

She could see her students grappling with the concept, their expressions a mix of intrigue and bewilderment. Ms. Patel realized she needed to ground this abstract idea in something more tangible.

"Let's try an exercise," she suggested, her voice infused with enthusiasm. "Imagine you're a gardener, and your life is the garden. In some religions, you might be given a strict plan – plant roses here, tulips there, water twice a day. But in *Sanatana Dharma*, you're given seeds, soil, and general knowledge about gardening. Your task is to create a garden that thrives in your specific climate, with your unique resources."

She drew a simple garden on the board, illustrating how different factors could influence a person's *dharma*.

"Your garden – your *dharma* – might look very different from your neighbor's. And that's okay. The goal isn't to have identical gardens, but to have gardens that are healthy, beautiful, and in harmony with their environment."

Ms. Patel saw understanding begin to blossom on some faces, like the first buds of spring. She was more than overjoyed that she burned midnight oil the past weeks. She extended the garden analogy and pushed the class a wee more to flex their intellectual muscles.

"Suppose I tell you a rule, *don't kill.* How would you apply that as a rule versus, if I had told you, it was a guideline?" she challenged.

"I will have to change my lifestyle immediately and become a vegetarian." rued Mike.

Lots of heads nodded together looking approvingly at Mike.

"And what practical difficulties you will encounter?" she persisted.

"Being a meat-eater, I will have to stop eating meat completely. That is very difficult for me. And I don't like vegetables. Also, I will have to stop working out as I will not get enough protein from vegetarian diet." Mike, a smart kid answered truthfully.

"But *don't kill* does not mean just animals alone." a small voice came from the far end of the room. All turned to look who was talking. It was Prema, with a forehead dot that seemed to twinkle with mischief and match the dance of the lovely golden earrings her grandmother had gifted her on her sixth birthday.

"That's true. I never thought of that. "Well, such a rule basically will make me stop eating completely." Said Mike and he continued," and I will die."

That's when Ms. Patel prodded the class with another googly. She asked, "What if we interpret that as a guideline, instead of a rule?"

"Then it becomes easier to implement. We will live and let live. We will end up making different choices without guilt. We can for example, reduce the frequency of meat-eating." Said Mike. He was liking these discussions.

"But then how would we decide if we should eat meat, fish or vegetables, using this guideline?" asked Prema.

Ms. Patel brought back the concept of *dharma* and explained. "*ahimsa* is the name of the value that we must cultivate. The word is a compound word which means 'no-killing' or if you take other definitions of the first letter *a*, it also means 'less harm'. And, when we make our choices, we must be adopting those actions that cause the least harm for that situation. In this example of eating, since plants are the lowest element in the food chain, both for animals that we eat as well as for us, it makes sense to eat plants instead of animals. Also, the plants have lesser sensory development compared to the animals."

"I know this seems complicated compared to the clear-cut rules we've seen in other religions. But let's think about why this approach might be valuable. Life is complex, isn't it? It's not a straight road, but a winding path through a dense forest. What's right in one situation might not be right in another."

She paused, letting the metaphor sink in.

"By providing guidelines rather than absolute rules, *Sanatana Dharma* encourages people to think critically, and act wisely based on their specific circumstances. It's like giving someone a Swiss army knife instead of a single tool – it might be more complicated to use, but it's far more versatile."

Ms. Patel noticed several students nodding thoughtfully, their initial confusion giving way to curiosity.

"Imagine if we had a rule that said, 'always tell the truth'. Sounds good, right? But what if telling the truth would put someone in danger? *Sanatana Dharma* recognizes that life isn't always black and white. It's a vibrant tapestry of countless shades, and it trusts individuals to navigate this complex weave." She drew a tapestry on the board, with threads of various colors intertwining in intricate patterns.

"Each thread in this tapestry represents a decision, an action, a moment in your life. The colors might represent different virtues or priorities – truth, compassion, duty, personal growth. In some faiths, you might be told exactly which color to use for each thread. But in *Sanatana Dharma*, you're the weaver. You choose which colors to use where, creating a unique pattern that represents your journey through life."

The bell rang, startling everyone out of their contemplation. As students began packing up, Ms. Patel offered a final thought.

"This approach might be more challenging," she concluded, her voice carrying over the rustle of bags and papers. "It's like being asked to compose a symphony instead of just playing notes on a page. But it also respects our ability to reason and adapt. It acknowledges that what's right can depend on context. In a complex world, sometimes flexible guidelines can be more logical and practical than absolute rules."

As her students filed out, many deep in thought, Ms. Patel felt a sense of accomplishment wash over her. She had hoped to have guided them through the choppy waters of this complex concept, and while they might not have reached the shore of complete understanding, she saw in their eyes the spark of curiosity, the desire to explore further.

She smiled to herself, hoping she had not just explained Sanatana Dharma, but had planted seeds of appreciation for its nuanced approach. As she erased the board, wiping away the drawings of gardens and tapestries, she knew that the real lessons – the understanding of life's complexity and the importance of personal responsibility – would remain, growing and evolving in her students' minds like the very concept of *dharma* itself.

Sometimes, taking up the challenge to teach someone is a good learning opportunity. Ms. Patel reflected. *If I had not listened to those discourses of Mahabharata, I am sure I would have talked to the class about the three hundred and thirty million gods Hindus have, and the various complicated and often conflicting rituals.*

Present-Continuous and Not Past-Perfect

Tejas, a whirlwind of youthful skepticism, slammed his textbooks shut. "These epics, *Avva*," he declared, using the affectionate term for grandmother, "they're just stories, right? There's no proof they ever actually happened!"

Saraswati, a woman whose eyes held the wisdom of decades, chuckled. "Prove they didn't happen, Tejas," she countered, her voice laced with amusement.

Tejas, with the trademark Tejas-sharpness, scoffed. "The burden of proof lies with those making the claim, *Avva*! Where's the archaeology? The carbon dating?"

Saraswati raised an eyebrow. "And where," she countered gently, "is the evidence to definitively disprove millennia-old stories passed down through generations?" She decided it was time to teach what was usually not taught in school.

Tejas sputtered, momentarily caught off guard. "Well, that's..."

"Exactly," Saraswati smiled. "Science, my dear Tejas, is a powerful tool, but it's not infallible. It's constantly evolving, uncovering new truths that shatter old paradigms. Who knows what discoveries the future holds?"

Tejas, intrigued now, leaned forward. "So, you're saying there's a chance the *Mahabharata* and *Ramayana* could be true?"

"There's always a chance, Tejas," Saraswati said. "But the true value of these epics lies not in their historicity, but in the *Sanatana Dharma* principles they explain to the reader who wants to learn something valuable." She paused, and added, "To live a harmonious and contented life."

"*Sanatana Dharma*?" Tejas echoed, a new term sparking his curiosity.

"The eternal law, that is not easy to implement correctly yet extremely obvious if only one were looking for that with the right mindset" Saraswati explained. "The *Mahabharata*, with its tale of duty, honor, and the consequences of unchecked ambition, teaches us about *Dharma*. The Ramayana, a story of unwavering devotion, love, and the triumph of good over evil, exemplifies the same principles. If you are looking for evidence buried deep underground in *Kurukshetra* to figure out if the *Mahabharata* war happened or the *Ram-Setu* that Lord Rama built with the help of an army of monkeys, bears and squirrels, you are looking for the wrong thing in these scriptures." She spoke.

A quizzical look clouded his eyes, brows knotting themselves together.

"These *puranas* do not care to produce objective evidence or leave hints & signs for future generations to determine authenticity of the events. Their purpose was to teach how to live harmoniously in this universe. Whether they happened or not is secondary – it is for the archaeologists, historians and linguists to create and present their theories with supporting evidence. The metaphors and the teachings that fill these stories indicate a simple, consistent fact – that the reader can't think of themselves separate from this universe. They need to think of themselves as part and parcel of this universe. When they think of themselves separate, a set of values emerge that would be different from when they consider themselves as part of the universe. Those values drive their behavior and life. The attempt in these stories is to make the reader see a sense of unity and interdependence in the universe and in turn help them understand that they are not only part of the problem, but they also have the power to solve the problem too."

This was surely a different perspective of looking at these scriptures. Tejas had always questioned their validity, but never considered that they were meant for a different purpose altogether.

Tejas pondered this. "So, it's not just about some larger-than-life characters fighting wars?"

"We can't be sure," Saraswati said. "These stories are like mirrors reflecting the human condition. They offer timeless lessons on how to live a meaningful life, how to navigate the complexities of relationships, and how to uphold *dharma* even in the face of adversity."

A thoughtful silence descended upon them. Tejas, the ever-questioning young man, began to see beyond the fantastical elements of the epics. He understood that science, while crucial, wasn't the only path to knowledge.

"Maybe," Tejas finally admitted, "I should approach these stories with a more open mind. Look beyond the literal and see the message they hold."

Saraswati beamed. "Excellent, Tejas! A good scientist is always open to possibilities, especially when dealing with the vast unknown. Remember, science is a journey, not a destination. It is present-continuous. But the past is perfect if you view these stories for the real purpose they were meant. Even a few millennia down the road, humans will continue to struggle with the same problem of discontentment, desire, anger, greed and will make bad choices. These stories will teach even our future generations the same what was taught to our ancestors few thousands of years ago. "

Tejas, with a newfound respect for the wisdom of his grandmother and the epics he once dismissed, decided to embark on a different kind of exploration – a journey into the heart of *Sanatana Dharma*, a philosophy as vast and enduring as the stories themselves.

The curious scientist in him decided it was time to apply the critical thinking skills to figure out what these stories were teaching us about harmonious living with the universe.

Paradox of Ahimsa

Vikrant was immensely happy that his short article was published in the leading newspaper. He had been pondering about the impossible paradox and felt that writing about it will give clarity and maybe reading comments to his article will help him identify blind spots that he may have missed. Afterall, *ahimsa* is not an easy value to follow. Impossible to follow in this world.

Ahimsa's Impossible Paradox by Vikrant Sharma

Ahimsa Paramo Dharmah – Non-violence is the supreme duty. This cornerstone of *Sanatana Dharma*, Hinduism's eternal path, has left me grappling with an existential crisis. Every action we take, every breath we draw, disrupts the delicate balance of life around us. From the insects crushed underfoot to the plants we consume; our very existence necessitates violence.

Can true adherence to *Ahimsa* then, coexist with life itself? Logic dictates that the only way to uphold this principle flawlessly is through self-termination. By ending one's own life, the cycle of violence ceases. It's a radical solution, yes, but isn't the pursuit of ultimate non-violence worth the ultimate sacrifice?

I understand the social and emotional upheaval this proposition might cause. But isn't causing emotional distress to loved ones a lesser evil compared to the constant, visible and direct violence we inflict on the world with every breath we take, every move we make and every action that we do or even don't do?

The concept of *Ahimsa*, as I see it, presents a paradox. To live is to inflict harm. Perhaps, the most *'ahimsa'*-ful act is to choose the path of least harm: to extinguish the flame of life itself and achieve true non-violence in death.

His article got too many comments. Some praised him for his puritanical and rational idea. Some others condemned him. Called him names. Stupid. Idiot. Convoluted. Crazy etc.

Few weeks went by, and the editor told him they were running another article by an Indian monk the next week and asked him to read the counter view.

Ahimsa – A Dynamic Embrace, not a Static Edict by Swami Omkar Ananda

Vikrant Sharma's article, while raising a valid philosophical question, presents a skewed interpretation of *Ahimsa*. *Sanatana Dharma* is not a religion of rigid rules, but a living philosophy that adapts with time. *Ahimsa*, the principle of non-violence, remains constant, but its application evolves.

To interpret *Ahimsa* only in the context of 'killing' other beings, which is necessitated by the very act of living is but a narrow view of the vast spectrum of how and where *Ahimsa* needs to be applied. It is not just about physical harm, but about non-physical violence in thought, word, and deed. But let us first explore why choosing to end one's life to uphold *ahimsa* is a flawed argument. Suicide is an act of violence – to oneself, and to the loved ones left behind. If one must be true to the principle of *ahimsa,* one must be able to follow and apply in all situations, to all people, all beings and in all times. The author has argued that ending life is the least harmful decisions to make. But this is not following the principle truthfully, even according to his own interpretation! Because if one were to be truthful to that principle of *ahimsa,* then they would be striving to find a solution not to harm even themselves. They would not kill themselves even if they consider their life less worthy than the very bacteria and virus that they are annihilating with every breath.

Therefore, it is my firm belief that the author has not logically thought through what this principle means. In our tradition, we give foremost importance to life of all forms. We accept that every life form has its place in this grand happening in the universe, whether we know and understand it or not. Therefore, true *ahimsa* lies in navigating this world with compassion, minimizing harm at every turn, and not always interpreting the guideline wrongly as *no harm, to all beings.* That is simply illogical.

Next let us debate an ethical dilemma. Does anyone have the legitimate right to take a life without the power to create one? The author's parents did not have the power to create life either. They were just instruments to come together to channelize life during birth. Therefore, the author's argument that ending life is the best solution is ethically not tenable.

Let us now debate about the spectrum where and how this principle needs to be applied. How often do we know the impact of our words on others? They say that science is learning to understand that even plants cringe when we use harsh words while talking to them. Has the author even considered *ahimsa* in speech? Pushing this argument further back, any action – be it physical or verbal must follow a thought. Whether we know the thought or not, the emotion or not, if we are acting or talking, there is one. No effect without cause. So, violent actions and violent speech are caused by violent thoughts. It is another way of saying in the American way – the thought matters! Should not the principle of *ahimsa* apply to our thoughts?

Finally, I also want to present a linguistic argument. Understanding the principles of a culture must be attempted from their point of view. The ontology, epistemology and theology of that culture are very important. A culture is best understood only when we understand and interpret the language of that culture correctly. The word *ahimsa* is wrongly interpreted as *non-violence* in English, which by itself alone, could be the cause of the author's confusion. The *Sanskrit* word, *ahimsa* is made of two simple words *a & himsa*. Dictionary definition of '*a*' will show us six meanings – complete negation (*non*) and partial negation (*least*) are valid meanings. Choosing which meaning to use now becomes contextual. And to understand the context, one needs to study the different stories told in epics like *Ramayana & Mahabharata* as to how the word *ahimsa* was used by different people in their lives. That is true learning from the context and taking the right meaning. Blind translation and consequent interpretation will most likely lead to wrong conclusions.

Vikrant wrestles with a genuine question, but his solution stems from a huge misunderstanding. *Ahimsa* is not a death wish, but a dynamic embrace of life, lived with utmost care and respect for all beings. If that principle must be applied successfully in life, then it requires intelligent living to determine least harm in every action. I would strongly encourage the author to better understand the context from the scriptures and not rely on linguistic inferences.

Vikrant was shocked. Pleasantly surprised that the monk offered a long rebuttal to his very short article. The monk's logic was flawless. He called the editor a few weeks later and requested them to publish his article expanding on his understanding of *ahimsa*.

A Mea Culpa and a Renewed Path by Vikrant Sharma

Swami Omkar Ananda's response to my article has been an eye-opener. In my quest for a logical solution, I blinded myself to the essence of *Ahimsa*.

My argument, framed in absolutes, failed to acknowledge the beautiful complexities of *Sanatana Dharma*. *Ahimṣa* is not a binary choice between life and death, but a spectrum of actions guided by compassion and a constant effort to minimize harm. This is a big difference that I as a convent educated person, with little knowledge of the deeper meanings of *Sanskrit* words, did not know before.

Swami Omkar Ananda rightly points out that my proposed solution – ending life – is itself an act of violence. I had become so fixated on the theoretical 'perfect' *Ahimsa* that I lost sight of the practical application of minimizing violence in our everyday lives. This guideline also helps to navigate the complexities of our personal situations by asking the question, *what is the right thing to do?*

I am grateful to Swami Omkar Ananda for challenging my flawed logic and reminding me of the true spirit of *Ahimsa*. My journey towards understanding this principle continues, and I am now armed with a deeper perspective. For all those others who have commented on my article, I am not following the path of Reddit anonymous polls that ask the audience to tell them their solution to a challenging life situation, and then follow the solution majority approve. I did get many agreements to my original post, but I will follow what Swamiji says, and not your collective advise.

Thank you, Swami Omkar Ananda, for helping me see the path forward.

Conversion Ki Kahani

Ram screamed. Sita was in the kitchen and heard him loud. It was a blood curdling scream. She dropped the *paneer paratha* on the *tava* and rushed upstairs, hoping that Ram had not hurt himself. He had gone up to clean up Swati's room.

They had just dropped her at the airport in the morning for her final semester.

Sita was aghast to see what Ram was holding on to. A small prayer mat and a *Koran*. That explained everything to her.

Swati had been acting strangely the past few months. Occasionally, she would go off to her room and lock herself in for some time. And, she also had started wearing those *salwar kameez* more often at home than the usual shorts & T's that she was quite comfortable with. Even when the weather was warm, she was using her *dupatta* to cover her hair.

Sita's knees felt weak, and she collapsed on the floor. Ram rushed to hold her and made her lie down on the bed.

"*Yeh kya hua?* I don't understand. Call her and we should talk with her."

"Give it a few more hours. She is on the flight now. Let us call her around noon and she would have been at the hostel." Ram said.

They started going through the room and found that Swati had forgotten a small cardboard full of stuff. Stuff they had never seen before. Pamphlets, paraphernalia, *burqah*, *hijab* and so on.

The phone rang. It was Swati.

"Mama, I forgot something in my room, and I think you may have discovered what it is by now." She slowly spoke.

"Why Swati? What do you know about Islam that you started practicing the religion?" Sita asked.

Ram was listening on the speakerphone.

"*Ho gaya Mama.*" She was casual. Said those words like a statement of fact. That hurt badly. Both Ram and Sita could not take the pain. Tears rolled down both their eyes. "I was searching for answers and found them here." She added.

The tears swelled. Swati was indeed a curious kid. She had asked a lot of questions. Ram and Sita had not answered. They had their reasons. They envisioned a life for her where she saw all religions were either equally important or equally unimportant. As parents they both emphasized logical, rational, scientific thinking in Swati. They taught her to separate religion from science. They were not always successful to bring up in such a sterile atmosphere. Outside influences – friends and their families, their beliefs always played a role in Swati's upbringing. And, Sita-Ram duo could not control those influences.

And she had questions. So many of them. That they could not answer.

What was there before the Big Bang?

Can something come out of nothing?

How can something be in two places at the same time?

How can two people born at the same time, to the same parents have different lives?

What fault is it of the kid who is born with some deformity?

What happens at death?

What is mind? What is brain? What is the difference?

Why do we have so many gods?

What is heaven? What is hell?

Does rebirth make sense? Is it scientific?

Why is there discrimination in the form of caste?

Why don't we have a community? Social circle?

We don't belong to anywhere. No one comes to our house, neither we go to anybody else's. Why?

What scripture tells us how to live our life correctly? It seems very confusing. There are no clear directions.

They both wanted to bring up their daughter 'secular', without any affiliation to any religion. Sita was a Rajputani and Ram was a Tamil Brahmin. They had met in their under-grad at college and after a whirlwind of romance had married and were living happily till Swati's teen years. Their tacit pact to bring up Swati irreligious seemed to have backfired. Swati was naturally curious. But neither Ram nor Sita knew much about their own culture, customs, traditions. Ram had thrown away the *janeu* the first time he drank from the bottle. He did not believe in any of these. Seemed totally unscientific. They brought up Swati to enjoy the festivities, food, movies, clothes – and travel to different destinations each holiday.

"But did you even consider our own religion Swati?" an agony from Ram, guiltily came out in the form of words. He half believed what he said, but his mind was caught with a swirl of emotions that he did not know how to handle. He did not even know the meaning of the words he used, *our religion*. He probably sounded like a politician speaking vacuous words.

"Yes, I have. Neither you nor Mama have been able to answer my questions. I was always rebuked or ridiculed. You did not teach me what our religion meant. And, searching online, I only got more confused. When I met Salman, he made this path so much easy for me to follow." Swati said.

"Who is Salman?" asked Sita, fearing the worst.

"My boyfriend. We met earlier this year at the gym."

Sita's loud wails drowned whatever Swati was saying. Finally, she hung up the phone, saying, "I will call you tomorrow."

The *paratha* on the *tava* had been completely burnt. Kitchen was full of fumes and the smoke alarm had gone off. Both rushed down. They could not figure out how to stop the damn noise from the alarm. Ram yanked the smoke alarm hard, and the sound stopped.

But they could still hear loud sounds coming from their blood pounding through the veins into their temples. Neither spoke. They had no appetite to eat anything. Sita went to the backyard. Her place. Ram knew. It just meant to him to leave her alone for some time.

He put on his shoes and decided to take a walk. He knew whom to call. A friend from his school days. Who had turned a *sannyasi*. Someone that he had always mocked for his deep religious inclination who threw away a fantastic career as a successful engineer to just go find himself.

"Krishna, I don't know what to do now. What did I do wrong?" he asked.

Krishna gently asked. "Will you permit me to be direct and truthful?"

He nodded his head and said yes.

"It could hurt" said Krishna and continued. "Remember the time when Swati was born and how forceful you were to bring her in a secular way? We had argued bitterly then. Something that you held against me for a long time too."

"Yes, I remember that. You had challenged me to first learn about our own religion, apply the smell test of logic to the principles it was propagating. And, I had told you that science and religion don't mix like water and oil. I had argued that religion was unscientific." Ram spoke.

The one person he deliberately started avoiding after Swati was born was Krishna. He had thought his ideas were radical and did not go well with their vision of future for Swati.

"Even today I want to tell you what I had told you then. It is never too late. Your kid is searching for answers. She has a goal in mind. You should adapt to your daughter's needs rather than pooh-poohing her inquiries into seeking answers. She has just gone astray a bit and will come back. Provided....." he stopped.

Ram was eager to hear what the key to the kingdom was.

"You start somewhere too. Your daughter will learn more from what you do…. than what you say" Krishna spoke the last part a bit more deliberately, emphasizing the importance of doing first, than preaching.

That was a tough thing for Ram to do. His forty-fifth birthday was coming up in two weeks and it would be difficult to bend a fully grown tree. *I am rigid and set in my own ideas.* But he knew that whatever he would say to Swati, she will know he was a fake.

Ram's dilemma was understandable. He knew as much about his own religion as much as he knew about Islam. Nothing. Yet, he was biased that his daughter had rejected a religion and chose another. It all now seemed illogical to dismiss something without even knowing anything about it. It was probably his ego that was hurt now. That led him on a guilt trip. He began questioning his parenting. Had he and Sita been wrong all along? *That's tough to accept. Swati is a fine girl, except for this.*

For several hours Ram listened attentively to Krishna. This time, there was no mockery. Krishna was making sense to him now. He shared the overall philosophy and explained how it made sense. Much more relevant than science, logic to live a harmonious and contented, purposeful life. Ram even had asked many challenging questions that Swati had asked him all along and he got answers from Krishna.

As he walked back home, Sita was waiting to catch him. He had by then noticed many missed calls from her.

"Ram, we should call Krishna for your forty-fifth birthday. Invite all your friends and ask him to tell us in simple way a bit more about Hinduism. Swati will also be here and maybe she will listen too, with an open mind."

"I was listening to him for the last two hours. That's why I did not pick your calls. Let's do it. That's a fantastic idea. But what he told me is important for us to follow. We can't force Swati now, but we can change. And, if we do, maybe she will see sense too."

"I will also be open-minded. Will listen attentively, research more and compare different religions. What I am concerned is that Swati could not even learn about our own religion. All fault of ours for having denied her the opportunity. Because of our rigidity."

The forty-fifth birthday came and went. All worked out according to the plan. But Swati continued her own path. Ram and Sita had begun to change though. And they planned to do the Kailash-Manasarovar yatra before Ram turned fifty. His knees were already begging him to drop the plan. But the pain that their daughter was not seeing what they are able to see now haunted him more than his knees. The pain also taught him patience and forbearance.

It was Ram's fiftieth birthday. They were overjoyed by what Swati asked them.

"I have been talking with Krishna-uncle ever since your forty-fifth. I know what the two paths offer. I have a better clarity now. Uncle was asking me to take a trip to Kailash. Can I come along with you both?"

He hugged her tight. And cried.

"I broke up with Salman a year back. It was clear that the other path was not the right one for me. But I was still not sure if this was the path for me. I now know the value of definitions and logical thinking. What I understood is that the definition of God is not same in all religions. I choose the definition of *Isvara* as most practical & beneficial. Also, now I am sure that any path that dictates moral absolutes is not practical."

Sita smiled at what she heard. Thoughts swirling in her heavy heart. *We had lost Swati these years. Probably eight or nine years. Approx one third of her life! She must have through so much stuff. Exploring all by herself. Being led away. Confusion. Trying to understand meaning of life. Boyfriend se Breakup Tak. Yet she never shared anything with us. It must have been stressful. We were not part of her life. She must have seen us as closed bigots.*

She suddenly felt jealous of the *sannyasi*. He was her daughter's confidante now. But Krishna was unaware of her looking at him. He was enjoying the delicious chocolate cake, while chatting animatedly with a bunch of friends and their children.

Great Poetry, No Substance

Three glasses of wine later, Satya became a performer. He was sharp as a tack and had a strong sense of logic and wit. Plus, an innate ability to express himself well. What his friends call as 'life of a party'. Any party he goes, the conversations become endless. He opines on everything with sound logic to support every opinion he held. With wine adding special effects to his performance, he becomes more banal, fun, insightful and sometimes cutely stupid – all at the same time.

Satya held court as usual that evening as well. His voice rising above the sixties rock music that was playing in the background. The topic was close to the heart of many people. All *desis* had assembled over the long weekend. In their early forties, they like to reminisce about their growing up times. Several went to college together and had a shared history. Same jokes repeated all the time, in every party, yet relished as new. All laughed at the same jokes, same episodes. Repeated with fidelity and no *masala* added. For over two decades, nothing changed. Except the depth of laughter and camaraderie within this group of friends.

"The *Vedas*? Mere epics," he declared, swirling his tea dramatically. "Great poems, perhaps, but nothing more. Homer's Iliad, now that's a story with substance! Our ancestors," he sighed, "wonderful bards, but lacked the depth, you see."

This was a familiar tune for his friends. Satya, a staunch believer in the Aryan invasion theory, viewed Indian history through a European lens. *Sanskrit*, he believed, was a gift bestowed upon the Indus Valley people by these fair-skinned invaders. There were weak debaters who gave up without refuting his logic. Over time, whenever the topic of Indian philosophy or religious culture came, everyone toed his line.

Smitha's young daughter, who just completed her middle school, was intently listening to the monologue and the vehement nodding of heads agreeing to him. She became curious. She asked, "Uncle, how can you disprove that these poems in *Vedas* lacked any depth? Did you read them?"

It was a genuine question but he was challenged. He felt he could road-roll her too like he did with his audience. The wine spoke perhaps. "Oh Yes, I have read *Purusha Sukta*. It is one of the first *Rg Veda* hymns. Very poetic – describing the God of *Hindus* in many ways. Head was *Brahmin*, shoulders were *Kshatriyas*, thighs were *vysyas* and feet were *sudras*. Loved the description but hated the outcome of it. The caste system was born in India because of this."

"Well. You are mistaken. I have watched some Youtube videos that explain the significance and deeper meaning of these hymns." She said and walked away as a friend pulled her for a game of cards in the other room.

Few months later, on an evening, over dinner, Satya found himself locked in a debate with his father, a man who, like him, had always scoffed at religion. After retirement his dad had started dabbling into ancient Indian history and ten years of consistent study. He had not only earned a PhD but was becoming a popular guest speaker at schools and colleges about what was not taught, yet essential. That was his full-time profession now. All for no money., that he would gladly do anytime.

But tonight, a flicker of something new danced in his father's eyes. "Satya," his father began, his voice unusually quiet, "Something I discovered a while back..." He hesitated, then spoke of a newfound fascination with *Sanskrit* – specifically, its structure, etymology, grammar & prosody. For three years, I have been learning *Sanskrit* here at *Samskrita Bharati* and am enjoying the nuances of the language.

Satya scoffed. "Prosody? Etymology? What good is that in the real world?"

His father smiled sadly. "It's the key to understanding the *Vedas*, Satya. It's called '*Chandas*', a whole branch of study dedicated to the rhythm and meter of the verses. It's what makes the Vedas so beautiful, so powerful." He explained how the very structure of the language allowed for immense flexibility in sentence construction, making it a poet's playground. "Think about it," he said, "word order doesn't matter in *Sanskrit*! You can rearrange the words and still retain the meaning perfectly. Imagine the freedom that gives a writer!"

His face still showed a *so what* to his dad. His dad continued. "Each word comes from a root word. The words have different meanings based on the context in which they are used."

"That's no different from any language dad." He protested.

"I agree it is not different. But think about a language – probably the only surviving language in the world today, that does not care about the word order. Would you think that such a language would have developed in a civilization that was primitive and barbaric? Would you think that these hymns were just beautiful poems with no meaning, without even trying to read them in their original version in *Sanskrit*? A simple word has atleast few pages of meaning in a dictionary. Those different meanings come from the context in which the words were used in the culture over time."

Satya became curious. He asked, "So, tell me about the word *Aryan*. What is its etymology?"

What his dad told him blew his mind off. He had never known. Intrigued, Satya delved deeper. He learned about the word "*Arya*," a term used in the *Vedas* to denote a noble person, someone of good character, not race. It was used to denote respect too. Importantly, he discovered that this was how the word was used in *Mahabharata* & *Ramayana*. He studied a bit more, diving into alternate histories of India rather than the popular narratives that had been taught since childhood. The West, he discovered, had appropriated this term – like the Nazis did with the *swastika*, twisting it into a justification for their theory of a conquering *Aryan* race. They had to find a way of pushing a narrative that Indo-European languages had the same European source. Unfortunately, there was no rock-solid evidence to this. He explored a bit more on 23&me on DNA evidence and concluded that it is difficult to peg with certainty which civilization came first.

Shame washed over him. His entire understanding of his own history had been built on a lie.

Three months of reading, understanding and exploring with an open mind was refreshing. He became quieter but very inquisitive. He had to validate one other thing and picked it up with his dad.

"The word *deva* is translated as God in English. Is that correct?" he asked.

His dad chuckled and said, "That is the problem you would face when you read translations. You are looking at words out of context and applying a known meaning from a different context to a new word. In this case, 'God' is a Western construct and embeds within the meaning derived from a Christian theology. However, *deva* just means 'that shines', coming from a root verb indicating 'to shine' amongst its many other meanings. So, these are not at all equivalent. We don't have an equivalent of Christian God in our culture. We don't understand God as apart from this universe we are in. Big difference *beta*."

That revelation was a turning point. Satya began devouring everything he could find on *Sanskrit*, on the *Vedas*. The more he learned, the more his perspective shifted. He realized that far from being primitive, his ancestors had possessed a sophisticated language and a rich literary tradition. The Vedas, he saw, were not just poems but a treasure trove of knowledge, philosophy, and scientific inquiry. He even doubted if these were written by a human – some alien powerful force must have written these *Vedas*.

He looked up the dictionary one last time before formally enrolling in a *Sanskrit* class. The very word *veda* does not denote a book, unlike the Bible or Koran. It simply meant, *'that which needs to be known'*. The entire body of knowledge is to explain that all pervasive, ever true conscious principle as our true nature and everything else as apparently true, but not quite. So simple, yet so powerful. No diktats, not a simplistic, deterministic path of a book. But lost in translation.

He joined *Sanskrit* classes, the ancient language no longer a relic of the past but a bridge to his roots. He started attending lectures on the *Vedas*, their complex symbolism slowly unraveling before him.

A decade later, in his fifties, Satya had embarked on a new journey – one of rediscovering his own heritage and educating the people. The man who once dismissed his own culture now championed it, his voice ringing out with newfound pride. The seeds of doubt his father had sown had blossomed into a garden of knowledge, a testament to the fact that it's never too late to learn, to unlearn, and to rediscover the richness of one's own heritage.

That little teen was his first *guru*, then it was his dad and the others. He smiled to himself that the word itself lends poorly to be translated as 'teacher', but translated correctly would mean someone (something) who (that) would remove darkness of ignorance.

Like a lamp lit, dispelling the darkness.

Aar Ya Paar

The muted glow of the bedside lamp cast long shadows on the bedroom walls. Maya lay curled up, her back to Rohan, the silence heavy with a shared burden. Rohan knew exactly what haunted her – the rasping cough that echoed from their last video call with *Amma* in Chennai. The once vibrant woman who used to fill the screen with laughter now looked frail and worn.

"Any sleep?" Rohan finally asked, his voice rough with worry.

"Just snatches," Maya whispered, turning towards him. Her eyes, usually sparkling with life, were red-rimmed and hollow. "How can we just be here while *Amma* struggles like that, so far away?"

Rohan sighed, the weight of their situation pressing down on him. Fifteen years ago, they'd left India, chasing the American dream – a secure future for their children, Akash and Diya, a better education, a life less burdened by the daily struggles they'd known. His startup in Bangalore had failed. He had lost almost everything. Their house was reclaimed by the bank. And he became unemployable. Companies hesitated to hire him thinking he would ditch them soon and get back to doing another startup. *An entrepreneur, always an entrepreneur. They have that keeda in them.* That was the constant refrain he heard from everyone. He was rejected by many companies. Finally, his boss from the last firm he worked for called him.

"Go to the US. Work for our client and manage the project. But you need to commit to stay back in US for atleast a few years and grow the account." He had said.

Back then, it had seemed like the right choice. He would not have found another job anyway for six months and that would have meant he would be deep in debt. Now, with Akash a college senior and Diya applying to colleges, leaving US felt like abandoning everything they'd built.

His parents had died when he was in college. The landslides that covered the path to Badrinath had taken the jeep along with it, into the deep crevices of Himalayas. Never to be found. He had become an orphan in an instant. With a meagre middle-class income his dad had taken loans on his provident fund, sold some shares to pay for his education. Still, it was not sufficient, and he had taken loans too. Few weeks after his parents' death, he had received a lien letter to all movable assets in their home and a demand notice from the bank to repay the loan back.

Maya and her mom came to his support. Maya and Rohan were already a pair for two years when his parents had died. All it took was a brief phone call from Maya to her mom. She had professed her love for Rohan and had told her the extenuating circumstances he was in. Aunty, that's how he had called her then, did not hesitate. She went to the bank the next day and paid off the loan. She took care of Rohan's one year of college fees along with Maya's. She was a superwoman. She was widowed at a very early age and continued to work as an administrative secretary in the Tamil Nadu government.

Auty had become *Amma* to him very soon. After they were married, *Amma* moved in with them soon. She could not wait till her retirement. She had developed cancer. It was in early stages, and it made her so tired daily that she had to call it quits.

"Do you think we were wrong, Rohan?" Maya's voice trembled. "Should we have stayed back?"

Rohan reached out, his hand hovering over hers before intertwining their fingers. "It's not that simple, Maya. Here, we can afford the best doctors for *Amma*. But she is adamant and does not want to leave India. And we had to come here, you know the reason why."

"But money can't replace us, Rohan," Maya choked back a sob, saddened by the fact that they were able to regularly send money to *Amma,* but were not there to physically help her. "She needs us. She needs a daughter now. Someone to take care of her. She is all I have. I don't even recall my dad. He has died much before I knew anything at all." She added, "*Amma* is stubborn, and it is not that we did not plead with her many times to move here to US."

"I know" he nodded his head, speaking softly.

Amma had stuck to a very simple decision. When Rohan and Maya were struggling financially, and the opportunity to relocate to US came about, she had encouraged them to go. "Don't worry about me," she'd reassured Rohan, "Focus on your work, on the children's future. Go there and stabilize yourself. Once you have become stronger financially, then you can think of coming back."

Life had been good ever since they came to the US. They survived one downturn, bought a home. Rohan had stayed with the same company. He could not move his job because of his H1 visa restrictions. Plus, the informal promise to his boss to take care of the firm. Few years became more than a decade. He continued to struggle with his visa situation and stayed put in his job. Maya preferred to be a homemaker, and she loved being one, occasionally teaching pro-bono to children in the neighborhood. But when they decided to buy their home, she too took up a job to afford the mortgage.

But the guilt gnawed at Rohan. His job, while secure, wouldn't allow for an extended leave. He couldn't risk jeopardizing their entire life here, not with Akash on the cusp of college and Diya's future hanging in the balance. Neither could they move back to India now. Kids had literally grown up in this environment and plucking them out was not an option. Plus, they had the house. Once a joy and pride of their life & success in US, it now felt like an albatross stuck to their neck. Maya knew all this. She knew that if she quit her job to go to India, they can't pay the mortgage., leave alone fund their kid's college.

"We're stuck, aren't we?" Maya whispered, a tear tracing a path down her cheek. "Stuck between two worlds, with no good choices."

Rohan pulled her closer, holding her tight. They sat in companionable silence for a long time, the weight of their situation a heavy presence in the room. There were no easy answers, just a desperate longing to be there for *Amma*, a yearning to rewind time and make different choices.

Finally, Maya spoke, her voice thick with emotion. "I wish someone tell me what the right thing is to do now. I seem to be stuck between the devil and the deep sea. If I go to India to take care of *Amma*, I am responsible for putting our family into financial trouble. And if I stay back here, I feel guilty of letting *Amma* be alone, especially with her failing health." She burst into cries.

Rohan held her tight. He did not know what the right thing to do was, either. Perhaps this was the *dharmic* dilemma that his old school friend was talking about. Two equally different choices, with severe consequences and one can't do without making a choice and living with the consequences.

The future remained uncertain, but in that shared moment of vulnerability, they found solace in each other's love, a love forged in sacrifice and a desperate hope that somehow, they could bridge the distance and mend the cracks in their hearts.

Maya hoped for teleportation. Rohan hoped for clarity.

Divorce Kyun Nahi?

Shilpa was sobbing. But he did not care. One loud crack. There was an immediate mark of his five fingers on her fair cheeks. It was if the blood flowed to her cheeks to support her moist eyes. She cried louder. In physical pain. *I can't endure anymore*, she thought.

Srinivas was sloshed. He had three pegs of whiskey neat, unleashing the animal inside him.

"*Saali,* you wanted to take Munnu and run away out of US?" he thundered.

Few minutes earlier, he had dragged her inside the home, with her clutching Munnu, their year-old girl. The immigration officials had called him. She had become a flight alert. A red alert had been in vogue in her name.

The immigration official had politely taken her and the baby to a secluded room and denied them to board. She was taken aback. She had asked why she could not board the flight.

"Your husband has gotten the courts issue an order. This order prevents you from leaving the country."

She was confused. How was it possible?

Srinivas' voice rang in her ears. His Hyderabadi accent sounding vulgar.

"I knew you will leave me and take the baby away from me. Thank God my complaint was fast tracked, and the airport did not allow you to leave. What were you thinking? Kidnapping Munnu and leaving US without my consent?"

The physical pain seemed dull, but the label of a kidnapper hurt her more. *Am I now a kidnapper of my own daughter?*

He snatched the baby from the floor and took her to the room upstairs, giving one hard kick to Shilpa on her stomach. She screamed again.

The next morning, she called Jyoti. The only friend who knew of her marital problems.

Srinivas and Shilpa were married for over a decade. She was from a wealthy, well-to-do family from Mulaparru village in the rice belt of Krishna River basin. He was from Hyderabad. Her parents were very happy to have found an *America abbayi* as a groom for her. They had sold twenty acres or more of fertile land, gave the dowry in cash and gold to get their only daughter married off and enjoy a great life in America. Sadly, they did not know.

Srinivas turned out to a drunkard, sadist and mean MCP. Shilpa lived a life of a maid, cook and cleaner during the day and whore at night. That's all he cared for. Chicken, biriyani, and sex. He took her passport and made her life worse than a slave.

It was good in the early days of their marriage. He was caring, romantic and she counted herself as a lucky girl. Till he learnt something about her. She had no way of deliberately hiding what would become the wedge in their marriage.

The fertility specialist had told them she can't get pregnant. Some reason that she did not understand. And the remedy for that would cost them upwards of quarter million dollars. Her trouble had started that very instant. But she never told anyone, except Jyoti.

"Can you ask your parents for some money?" Jyoti had suggested to Shilpa.

Shilpa called her parents, lied to them that Srinivas was starting a business, and he needed some capital. Her parents sold the reminder of the lands they had and wired her the money. She felt guilty but hoped that things will turn better.

Soon enough she was pregnant. Srinivas started becoming nice to her again and she started enjoying his attention. She forgot how horrible the past eight years were with him. After Munnu was born, his attention shifted towards the baby. He started ignoring her. It just took six months – going through post-partum depression, lack of empathy and attention from Srinivas, zero friends or support group; all had made her body change significantly. She gained over fifty pounds that she found it hard to shake off.

And the taunts got worse.

"Itni moti ho gayi. Lazy bhi. Jara ghar ka poora kaam sambal.[26]*"* Srinivas seemed to have just learnt one tune and this was it. Day in and day out, he made fun of her weight gain, made her guilty and forced her to do stuff like a slave.

---

26 'You have become too fat. And Lazy. Do household work properly."

One day when she could not take it anymore, she left home, along with Munnu. Jyoti picked her up. When Srinivas got back home, he was mad. He filed a police complaint about his missing wife and child. And the police were able to find her location and promptly returned her and the baby home. She had gotten the lashes from his worn-out leather belt that evening. Everywhere on her body.

And one day when she discovered where Srinivas had hid their passports, she made her plan. Borrowed money from Jyoti and booked tickets to go to India with the baby. Unfortunately, that plan had backfired and she was back in the mad lion's den yet again.

Then one day, her parents landed unannounced. They had been concerned that Shilpa had stopped calling them completely. They were missing Munnu's coos and baby smiles on Facetime. Whenever they called, Shilpa had never picked up.

She opened the door and was shocked to see them. They too were utterly in disbelief looking at Shilpa. Srinivas was not at home, and she poured out her heart.

Her dad asked her, "Why don't you divorce him?".

She spoke, "I would have. But for Munnu. She is but a baby. And he is a beast. Capable of doing anything. I don't trust him."

Her dad, although was not educated formally, was a man of wisdom. He was traditional and bound by customs and practices that he had grown up in. Marriage was a onetime affair in his culture, and divorce was unheard of. But he knew his daughter was torn between Munnu and her own freedom. He recognized that she was ready to slave her life for her daughter. Tears rolled down his eyes as he thought about the plight of his only daughter, brought up with such love and care, and living the most miserable life in the dream destination country. And, living scared to even complain.

Before Srinivas returned, her dad had decided. He told Shilpa his plan. She suddenly got the strength and saw sense in what her dad was saying. She wondered how she had missed this important insight all along. *Did she lack even the common sense not to see what to do?* She wondered silently. *Only I had the ability to pull up my socks. Amma, Nanna being here helped me strengthen my resolve to get out of this mess. It surely made my decision. Now, I need to go on the offensive. Be bold and tell everyone what violence I endured. Then work through the system to get rid of my travel restrictions. Get back home, recover.*

As the door opened, and Srinivas entered, he saw the cops sitting in his home. And his in-laws were there too. The cops read his rights and arrested him immediately. As he was taken away, Shilpa burst out crying. Yet again. But this time it was out of relief. And an opportunity to live a better life, with her daughter.

Her dad had just told her, "Happiness is like a cup full of water. It will overflow to other cups only when the cup is full. For your cup to be full you need to be free. Free of any stress. You will figure out your way. Let's go back to India. We are there for you." Jyoti, her only friend had supported her dad's idea and together they had called the cops. Shilpa recorded her statement of the torture she went through and had shown proof of the beatings.

She went upstairs and packed her suitcase, while Jyoti helped with booking tickets for her, her parents and Munnu. The court had ordered him to stay away atleast five miles away from the house for two weeks. Jyoti knew a good family lawyer who would get her travel restrictions lifted.

Two weeks later, when Srinivas returned to his home – everything was exactly there as it is. He noticed that a few cobwebs had not been cleaned, and dust had settled on his laptop and bookshelf. He turned around to kitchen and shouted, "Shilpa!" only to be met with a deafening silence.

Kanchi Karuna Katha[27]

Anup had envisioned his first family trip to India as a pilgrimage, a vibrant immersion into his heritage. He had a rock-solid reason for that. Somehow in his heart of hearts, he had this strong feeling that if one had to admire and understand India, temples are the window to an ancient living culture and civilization. He knew that 4M – Music, Movies, *Masala* and *Mufti* (he had coined the last terms to rhyme with the first two. His family knew what it meant – food and clothes) were just the first layer – an external representation of the magic called India. Truth be told, he was an eager beaver himself to dig into the temples of the past.

He was in his mid-fifties. Greying hair, wrinkles slowly visible under his chin, if one carefully looked at him. But those did not belie the sharp mind he was. His eyes give away his keen sense of logic, and incisive mind. He had a knack for reading huge amount of information in a short period, remember the details and connect the dots to create a cohesive, logical story. That's how he had made a name for himself in the New York law scene. For three decades he was a successful, most sought after corporate lawyer, having been employed by many firms across different industries.

---

27   *Kanchi* – Kanchipuram; *Karuna* – sorrowful; *katha* – story

Anup called New York his home. After the initial few years when he visited his parents regularly, he became disconnected to India. Work had consumed him. Moreover, as time consumed his parents, moving them into mere memories, he never felt the need to go back. It was two decades later that he was going now with his family. Two adult daughters who did not even look Indian in anyway. His girls had the knack to pick on their mom's genes. Anup's wife was from Estonia, and they had met when studying. It was obviously their first time to travel to India.

As the plane was touching down the Chennai airport, he jokingly assumed an air of superiority with his family. It was a family joke, that only the dad knew an Indian language. Or was atleast 'half Indian'.

"*Vanakkam* & welcome to Chennai" he imitated the air-hostess voice, and continued to say something in Tamil, while his daughters and wife were looking amused. His Tamil accent was heavily rusted.

Kanchipuram, Madurai, Chidambaram, Thanjavur and of course Chennai would be on the top of his list.

After a day's rest, accompanied by his oldest cousin Ramaswamy, who volunteered himself to chaperone them for the whole month, they drove to their first stop. Kanchipuram, the "City of a Thousand Temples," was impressive. Although the grand, ancient structures he'd seen in pictures were now faded and chipped, some with weeds pushing through cracks in the stone, there was beauty and culture. His effusive cousin, speaking in a mix of Tamil and English was sharing all he knew about each pillar of the temple. And the Kamakshi temple, being born from the myth of kings, *puranas* and *shakta* philosophy had many stories to tell – big and small. Ramaswamy had many connections in the temple and arranged for 'special' *darshan* for them. By evening, all four, exhausted from walking the long, intricately designed corridors, and admiring the intricate stone carvings, from where the patterns for the famous Kanchipuram *sarees* originated, soon fell asleep. Three of them though were dreaming which pattern *saree* to buy when they would go shopping soon.

They had miles to cover the following day. Surrounding the main Kanchi temple, there were many small temples, several of them dating back to late sixth century AD. The Pallavas were great builders. And there was especially one temple that he had wanted to take his family. Small but significant and he remembered that the idol there had a raised foot, as if it was measuring the skies. He wanted to relive his childhood memories too.

They all landed at the *Ulagalandha Perumal* temple, a simple, single-storied structure, the disappointment morphed into frustration. Ramaswamy had told them to get ready early so that they can beat the heat and go around many temples. This temple was to be wide open at 9AM, but the clock showed thirty minutes past nine and still it was shut. The family had waited for what it seemed like ages. But there was no sight of anyone opening the doors. They started looking around and were appalled to see the decrepit conditions the temple was in.

Finally, when a weary priest finally appeared, lugging a bucket of water, Anup couldn't contain his question. As the priest unlocked the door, Anup asked him.

"The temple was supposed to be open for *darshan* by 630AM. We have been waiting for *Perumal* darshan since an hour. Where were you, *Swami*? And why are the temples in such disrepair? Where do all the donations go?"

He had memories of his childhood temple visits. They all seemed huge, beautiful and well maintained. Not anymore.

The priest, a kind-faced man with worry etched in his forehead lines, sighed. "Very little comes to us, sir. We have hardly any funds. We priests are asked to even double up our duty and serve *Perumal* in the nearby temple. Did you go there? The one just hundred meters away? I was coming from there. They say it's government orders."

Anup's legal mind whirred. "Government orders? Why does the state control the temples?" He did not know that.

The priest shrugged, his gaze flickering to the worn idol within. "They say it's for better management. But sometimes…" He trailed off, a flicker of defiance in his eyes. "Sometimes, serving the Lord feels secondary to following their rules."

Anup's frustration deepened as he listened to that priest. His eyes fell on two huge brass keys that hung from the waist stuck to his *dhoti*. As if the priest noticed him, he continued. "We can't stop daily *puja* to *Perumal*. I am the only priest for two temples. When I am at the other temple, I lock this one and go there. And come back here after locking the other one. Usually someone or the other tell me if the devotees are waiting. But today nobody informed me." He reeled out his frustration in pure Tamil.

Then he continued, "Even without money, how can we let go of our daily traditions? Daily *abhishekams* need water. I go and fetch the water myself because I have no help. I have asked the administration for a tap here, but it is over six years, and I am still carrying daily pails of water."

He was not done. He lowered his voice as if he was afraid, "I don't have money to offer *Pongal* to the Lord on some days. But since the tradition must continue uninterrupted, my wife cooks at home and I offer it to the Lord. There are days when my salary has been delayed and I struggle to make my ends meet." He was smiling sadly saying this. He knew of the repercussions if his employers – the government learnt about what he said. He knew who his true employer was though and did not hesitate to tell the truth. Just as he did not hesitate to serve his employer every day, knowing well what his duty towards that *Perumal* was.

Anup was shocked. In the US, religion and state were clearly separate. The government did not have any say in the affairs of the religious institutions. These entities even enjoyed a lot of tax benefits. In India, it seemed totally opposite. He found it strange that places of worship were managed by government administrators who had no clue of the *sampradaya* of each temple deity. In all this, the priest's dedication to his duty stood out. How he explained the simple fact that the idol was a living God revealed itself in his unflinching commitment to offer the daily *naivadyam*.

Anup soon discovered this wasn't an isolated incident. Many temples, grand and small, suffered from neglect. He saw proof of it as they went around other temples. There were huge growth of weeds in one temple and homeless people sleeping in another. The lone lighted lamp was the only indication that it was an active temple still.

When he persisted to learn more asking questions to every priest, he got another shocker. Mosques and churches seemed to thrive, independent and well-maintained. Without governmental controls. Why so? He could not make out. A gnawing suspicion took root. Was it mismanagement of temple money, or something more sinister? Why was the special treatment given only Hindu temples?

The month-long trip was fun for his family. They bought lots of stuff – *sarees*, antiques, brassware, a lot of ethnic stuff and ate at different places – *idlis*, *vadas*, *dosas* of several varieties with *chutneys* of different kinds and *sambhar*. He enjoyed the trip too. But his objective had changed the very instant he had the dialogue with the first priest who opened his mind to the problem of temple funds and governmental control. He probed further to make understand if Kanchipuram temples were anomaly. Yet, the narrative was the same in Madurai, Thanjavur, Chidambaram and Chennai.

Back in New York, a fire ignited within Anup. He delved into legalities, and history. His days were filled with research and late nights strategizing about what he would do. The more he learned, the angrier he became. The state, claiming to protect them, was siphoning temple funds, stifling their autonomy. This wasn't just about crumbling structures; it was about killing the soul of his heritage softly and deliberately. He understood the nexus between land grabbers, religion, the politicians and state.

As he dug deeper, he realized the profound impact of invasions of the past. He had not known about these deep inflictions during his school days. Muslims and Christians had invaded, and ransacked the temples. He learnt of the struggle Hindus had to go through to protect their temples, idols and sacred space. Many families had even given up their life to protect the idols. For the first time, he understood why there was a fight for centuries to construct Ram temple in Ayodhya. And he understood why Tirupathi temple was a coveted prize for any political party in power. Or the reports about the immense hidden treasure in Padmanabha Swamy temple in Trivandrum and the public interest to protect the wealth from falling into the hands of the government.

He decided to do something about it.

Anup, the once corporate lawyer, transformed into a passionate advocate. He set up a charity, "Temple Liberation," dedicated to freeing temples from state control. He used his legal expertise to fight for temple rights, his voice resonating in courtrooms and on social media. He rallied the Indian diaspora, igniting a movement that transcended borders. He partnered with non-profits that worked to influence Britishers and other invaders to return the idols that they had stolen from our temples. He worked with lawyers, many of whom were branded as 'right wing' in the press – both in India and US to bring about change. A change to build not just pride but legal action and political lobbying to free temples from governmental controls. He advocated the public to be vocal and critical of the administrators, holding them accountable for every rupee spent. He turned on the heat.

Anup's journey wasn't easy. He faced opposition from entrenched bureaucracies and accusations of saffronization. But with each victory, a temple regained its independence, a flicker of hope rekindled. He envisioned a future where temples, free from state control, could flourish again, becoming vibrant centers of worship and cultural preservation.

Anup's fight was for the soul of his heritage. It was a fight to ensure that the ancient chants and traditions, the very essence of his culture, continued to echo through the ages, unburdened by the chains of control.

One day in an interview, he was asked to explain the logo of his charity.

"Oh, the background is the image of a two temple *gopurams*, adjacent to each other and in front of it is a weary priest walking from one temple to the other, carrying a pail of water."

Gaddar!

Priya and Riya, two childhood friends who grew up together, fiercely competed in all things – school, sports and competition. But they remained good friends. Gentle banter occasionally taking on a serious tone. But never something that they could not talk and resolve.

It was one of those gentle banters that one day turned into a bitter Whatsapp battle. Priya's comments after she saw Riya's status message photos of the grand *Krishna Janmashtami* celebrations that she organized in the local temple.

Riya paced back and forth in their small living room; her face flushed with anger. She had just received a WhatsApp message from Priya, her childhood friend from India, that had struck a nerve. Priya had taunted her about professing her love for Indian culture and Hinduism while living as a citizen of the United States.

"How can you be so proud of your *desi* heritage," Priya's message had read, "while willingly giving up your Indian citizenship? It's like living a double life, a fraud." What hurt Priya most was the word she had used, *gaddar. How can she call me a traitor?* Priya's words were hurting. Every time she picked up the phone to call her, she was worried about burning bridges with her.

It was a strong accusation from a close friend. She had never expected that. Moreover, she had never considered herself a fraud. She loved her Indian roots, her culture, and her religion. She was known to be a born organizer of events and volunteered at the local temple. But she also loved the opportunities and freedom that her American citizenship afforded her. She didn't see these two aspects of her life as mutually exclusive. Now, she was tormented by how her bestie was perceiving her. Her opinion mattered to Riya somehow.

"Sandeep," she finally turned to her husband, her voice trembling. "Priya is saying I'm a hypocrite."

Sandeep, a calm and patient man, sat down beside her. "Can you tell me exactly what Priya said?" He knew Priya well enough and her friendship with Riya to know that all will be OK finally, but it was his job to manage her emotions today. She was never this agitated in the past few months.

Riya repeated Priya's message. Sandeep listened carefully; his eyes closed in concentration.

"Riya," he began, his voice gentle, "I understand why you're upset. Priya's words are hurtful, and they're based on a misunderstanding."

"A misunderstanding?" Riya echoed; her voice filled with disbelief. "She's saying I'm not being true to myself."

Sandeep explained. "Priya is confusing the concept of nationality with the concept of culture and religion. She's assuming that because you're an American citizen, you've abandoned your Indian heritage."

He continued, "We immigrated to this country for better job prospects; there is nothing wrong with that. Humans have been nomads historically. It is ok to be an economic immigrant. The trouble starts when we start proselytizing our culture here onto the local population. And fortunately, our *dharma* does not care. We just follow our culture as individuals and give the freedom to others to follow theirs. No imposition of any kind. That way, we are integrating well into a new society, yet not letting go of our own traditions and culture."

Riya nodded slowly. She brightened up with this perspective. "I see what you mean. But isn't it a bit hypocritical to claim to love your culture while living in a different country? You know that I am a proud *desi,* and how do I reconcile the fact that I don't live in India and still claim I am proud of our *desi* culture?"

Sandeep smiled. "Not necessarily. Culture and religion are not bound by geographical borders. *Sanatana Dharma,* for example, is a universal philosophy that can be practiced by anyone, anywhere. It's not exclusive to people born in India."

Riya's eyes widened. "So, I can still be a good Hindu even though I'm an American citizen?"

"Absolutely," Sandeep affirmed. "Your citizenship is a man-made construct. It doesn't define your identity or your beliefs. What defines you is your connection to the principles and values of *Sanatana Dharma.*"

Riya felt a weight lift off her shoulders. They had just received their citizenship after a long struggle. More than fifteen years! She had been so caught up in the idea of new national identity that she had espoused and had forgotten the true essence of her religion.

"Thank you, Sandeep," she said, hugging him tightly. "I was so confused."

Sandeep returned her hug. "It's okay, Riya. Sometimes, we all need a little perspective."

As Riya sat back and reflected on their conversation, she realized that Priya's criticism was based on a flawed assumption. *Sanatana Dharma* was not a nationalistic ideology; it was a spiritual path that transcended borders. All it said was, that the entire universe is pervaded by the same principle. There is unity everywhere, manifesting itself in many shapes, forms – some moving, some not, some with life, some without. And the goal of human was to discover their identity as that very principle. Where was the question of that entity being restricted to a geography like India? How can anyone assume that just by crossing the seven seas, one has abandoned their quest to own up their identity? And she, as a follower of *Sanatana Dharma*, was free to practice her faith wherever she chose to live. Amid the bustling NY city or in the calm serene national parks of Yosemite, chaotic Bangalore or serene Himalayas. It just did not matter.

The next day, Riya decided to respond to Priya's message. She typed a long response carefully, trying to convey her feelings without sounding defensive.

"Dear Priya," she wrote, "I understand why you're upset, but your assumption that my citizenship somehow negates my connection to my culture and religion is flawed. India is a political entity, but *Bharatiyata*, the essence of being *Bharatiya* is the deep philosophical core of India. Even before 1947, when there were many kingdoms, each with their own political agenda and ambition, they were united with this *Bharatiyata* despite waging wars for political gains. *Sanatana Dharma* is not a nationalistic ideology. Maybe you are confusing with words like *Hindutva*, right wing *Hindu* etc. These are political ideologies and have nothing to do with our *dharma* in its true sense. You may be conflating the two, just like equating Zionist movement to Judaism, or British to Christianity. This philosophy is a universal philosophy that can be practiced by anyone, anywhere. My love for India and its culture is not diminished by my American citizenship. It's a part of who I am, and it's something I cherish deeply."

She paused for a moment, considering her words. Then, she added, "Just because I'm living in a different country doesn't mean I've forgotten my roots. I continue to celebrate Indian festivals, cook Indian food, and connect with my family and friends back home. My love for India is as strong as ever."

Riya hit send, her heart pounding. She waited anxiously for a response, but none came. She decided to let it go. Whether Priya understood her point or not, she had been true to herself. And that, she knew, was the most important thing.

The next day Priya called. She apologized for her remarks, and they laughed it off together.

Naseeb, Kismet Ya Karma?

No sooner the server dropped the beers on their table, the two got talking. The aroma of sizzling kebabs from the neighboring table filled the air as Naren and Ranveer settled into their usual dinner spot. Naren had called Ranveer to discuss something important.

"I got laid off today" spoke Naren. He gulped down the beer hoping that he will stop tearing. But his eyes gave him away. Ranveer noticed the shiny drops in his eyes. He said nothing.

Naren continued, his voice laced with a hint of bitterness. "I'd worked hard, given my all to that company. And yet, I was the one who got the pink slip. How can you explain that? Am a bit lost. I had always thought that we have one hundred percent control over our lives. And I did everything. Still…."

Ranveer was still silent, letting Naren pour out his disappointment and frustration. His confusion started to come out in his voice. "I thought it was always all about free will. Our choices, our actions, they shape our destiny. But it does not seem so."

Ranveer had held the exact opposite view of Naren. He countered, "I am so sorry Naren. Its fate, man. But I am sure you will find a new job. Much better paying too. *Hamare*

Naseeb mei kya likha hai[28], that's what is going to happen. *Kismet* seems to be the driving forces behind our lives. We're mere pawns in a grand cosmic game."

Their disagreement was nothing new. Naren was a firm believer in the power of individual choice, while Ranveer saw life as a predetermined journey. Tonight, however, their differing perspectives seemed to be colliding with a newfound intensity. Naren was confused. He suspected he had probably not given his one hundred percent…

Naren scoffed. "The job market is bad. And it's already mid-November. Nobody hires till January. But the visa situation is challenging too." He was on H1B and needed to find another employer quickly else he would have to get out of the country. Naren had made Denver his home, but even after eight years, he was still on visa. He had bought a home just a month back and had a huge mortgage to repay.

"I think I will have to start winding down and move back." He said, finishing his beer and signaling the waiter to get another round.

"What did I do to deserve this Ranveer? As far as I know, I always did the right thing – worked hard, met all the deadlines, was proactive, team player…yet they laid me off. Is it my problem that the company lost a major client? Should I be penalized for that?" He vented.

Ranveer slowly responded. "I don't think we can control everything that happens to us. Yesterday someone honked at

---

28   'Whatever is meant to happen'

me. I was startled, and when I saw that guy give me a middle finger, I was angry. I lowered my windows and shouted at him. I was angry too. But I don't think I will blame myself for that. It was my *karma* that the fellow honked at me and made me angry. I had to respond; what choice I had?"

"Ranveer, your example is off. Are you telling me that I had no choice in losing my job? And was I meant to lose it? But why?" Naren asked.

Naren could not believe the absurdity of what he was hearing. *If it is happening to me, I must have done something. If good, then good must happen. If I have done bad, something bad should happen. As simple as it. Cause & effect. But I was doing everything right, so why did this happen to me?*

Their conversation continued; each man steadfast in their beliefs. Naren recounted stories of his past successes, attributing them to his hard work and determination. He provided evidence of his appraisals where his boss explained why he got that raise or what he appreciated most and gave him that promotion. Ranveer, in turn, shared anecdotes of misfortune, blaming them on the whims of fate.

As their heated exchange reached a crescendo, their close friend, Krishna, arrived. He took a seat at their table, a knowing smile playing on his lips. Both knew that this guy was different.

He began, his voice calm and measured, "I believe you're both missing the bigger picture."

Naren and Ranveer turned to him, their curiosity piqued.

"You see," Krishna continued, "the truth lies somewhere between your two extremes. Free will and fate are not mutually exclusive. They work together, like two sides of a coin."

Naren and Ranveer exchanged puzzled glances.

"Imagine a river," Krishna explained. "The river's flow is a metaphor for fate. It's a force beyond our control. But we, as individuals, have the free will to navigate that flow. We can choose to swim upstream, against the current, or we can let it carry us downstream. We can choose to do nothing too. What choice we would exercise is our free-will but expect the river to flow the way it wants to flow. That is the fate."

"So, you're saying we have only limited control over our lives?" Naren asked, his skepticism fading.

"Exactly," Krishna replied. "But that control is fairly limited, because most of it is given. Think of this metaphor itself. The river flow, its depth, current strength, all the dangers of water are given. Your body is given to you. Its strength or lack of it is given. You can only nurture what is given, for example learning to swim or choosing not to. We can't change the river's flow, but we can choose how we respond to it. And our choices, in turn, shape our destiny."

Ranveer, who had been listening intently, nodded. A bit embarrassed too. "So, it's not just fate. How do you explain when someone gets a windfall, say a lottery ticket?"

"If you don't even make the effort to buy the lottery ticket, you will never win. That is freewill to buy the ticket. If you have done adequate actions in the past to be the recipient of the lottery, then you will win. That is *fate.*, although I don't like to use that word. Neither I like to use the word, *kismet* or *Naseeb.* These three words are not in our tradition. We summarize everything with the word *karma.* It means two things – *karmaphala,* the fruits of our past actions – which is given to us, and *karma,* actions we do now – our choices.

"But how can we know what those past actions were?" Naren asked.

"You will not know," Krishna said. "Our past actions, not just in this life, but in countless past lives will fructify. Which ones fructify now is not known. It is kept secret and given to you at the right time."

Naren and Ranveer exchanged surprised looks. They had never considered the concept of past lives in their discussions.

"*Karma* theory," Krishna replied. "is essential to explain the differences we see in our lives. I don't think there is any other elegant theory."

As Naren and Ranveer pondered Krishna's words, they realized that their debate had been based on a flawed understanding of reality. They had been trapped in a binary world, either believing in absolute control or absolute helplessness. But the truth, as Krishna had pointed out, was far more nuanced. They realized that extreme positions of any kind are always "non-thinking" positions, driven solely by pre-conceived notions and immaturity.

Naren, the man who had once believed in absolute control, began to see the limitations of his perspective. He realized that even the most carefully planned course of action could be derailed by unforeseen circumstances. He understood that sometimes, the best-laid plans of mice and men go awry.

Ranveer, on the other hand, began to appreciate the power of individual choice. He realized that while fate might set the stage, it was up to him to play the role. He could not control the circumstances, but he could control his response to them.

As they parted ways that evening, Naren and Ranveer felt a sense of newfound understanding. They had learned that life was not a black-and-white affair. It was a tapestry woven with threads of destiny and free will, each influencing the other in intricate and unpredictable ways.

The very next day, Naren choose to set aside his disappointments and focused on beating the H1B clock. He became proactive and reached out to all his connects. Very soon, he landed a great job.

Likewise, Ranveer, who had been considering losing 30 pounds, enrolled in the gym membership and decide to move his body a bit.

Cultures, Invasions, and Identity

The warm glow of the bar enveloped Raj and Aadhav as they settled into a cozy booth, the clinking of glasses and soft chatter of patrons creating a backdrop for their conversation. The aroma of spiced chicken wings and sizzling paneer tikka wafted through the air, mingling with the rich scent of freshly poured craft beers. It was a typical Friday evening, a time for friends to unwind and share their thoughts on the world.

Raj took a sip of his beer, a local brew with hints of citrus, and leaned back, his eyes sparkling with enthusiasm. "You know, Aadhav, I really believe that immigration is one of the best things to happen to a society. It brings in fresh ideas, different perspectives, and a beautiful tapestry of cultures. Just look at the U.S.—it's a melting pot!"

Aadhav, swirling his drink, raised an eyebrow. "Sure, it's a melting pot, but what happens when that pot boils over? Think about the indigenous cultures that get lost in the process. The Native Americans, for instance, faced devastating consequences when European settlers arrived. Their way of life was nearly obliterated."

Raj leaned forward, intrigued. "But isn't that just a part of history? Cultures have always influenced each other. Isn't that how we evolve?"

"Evolve, yes," Aadhav replied, his tone serious. "But at what cost? The Spanish Inquisition is a perfect example. When the Spanish colonizers arrived in the Americas, they didn't just bring their culture; they brought violence, disease, and forced conversions. Entire civilizations were wiped out. The Aztecs and Incas had rich traditions, languages, and beliefs, all but erased in a matter of decades."

Raj nodded slowly, the weight of Aadhav's words settling in. "That's a harsh reality. But India is different. We've had our share of invasions—Turkish, Persian, Mughal, and British—but our culture has endured. It's like a river that flows, absorbing different tributaries without losing its essence."

"True," Aadhav conceded, "but let's not romanticize it too much. The Mughals, for instance, did impose their culture and religion. Many Hindus were forcibly converted, and temples were destroyed. It's like a garden where some plants are uprooted to make space for others. Yes, the garden remains, but some flowers are lost forever."

Raj took a moment to reflect. "That's a fair point. But look at how Indian culture has adapted. We've absorbed influences from various invaders and yet retained our core identity. The Mughal architecture, for instance, is a beautiful blend of Persian and Indian styles. The Taj Mahal stands as a testament to that fusion."

"Absolutely," Aadhav agreed, "but we must also recognize the danger of cultural dilution. While the Taj Mahal is magnificent, it's also a reminder of what was lost. The indigenous practices, the local languages, the rituals—if we don't actively preserve them, they could fade away, just like the languages of the indigenous tribes in the Americas."

Raj took another sip of his beer, contemplating Aadhav's words. "But isn't it a natural part of human evolution to adapt? Look at how we've embraced technology and globalization. Isn't that progress?"

"Progress, yes, but at what cost?" Aadhav countered. "In India today, many young people are more influenced by Western culture than by their own traditions. They don't understand the depth of their own heritage. It's like a tree that forgets its roots while reaching for the sky."

Raj leaned back, a frown creasing his forehead. "I see your point. But isn't it also about choice? People are free to adopt what resonates with them."

"Choice is important," Aadhav replied, "but it becomes problematic when people don't even know what they're choosing from. If you don't understand your own culture, how can you appreciate or critique others? It's like trying to enjoy a dish without knowing the ingredients."

Raj's expression shifted as he pondered the implications. "So, you're saying that the apathy of the Hindu population towards their own culture is a significant risk?"

"Exactly," Aadhav said, his voice gaining intensity. "Look at the way some Hindu festivals are celebrated today—more like a show for social media than a genuine expression of faith. People dress up, take pictures, and forget the significance behind the rituals. It's like wearing a costume without understanding the character."

Raj chuckled, "I guess that's true. But isn't that the case with many cultures? Aren't we all guilty of commodifying our traditions?"

"Perhaps," Aadhav conceded, "but the stakes are higher for a culture that has faced historical erasure. The Mughals and the British didn't just conquer land; they sought to reshape identities. I read this quote somewhere – *In India we have only two types of people – Hindus and people who were Hindus.* And now, with globalization, there's a risk of losing the essence of what it means to be Indian."

Raj took a deep breath, the gravity of the conversation settling in. "So, what's the solution? How do we ensure that our culture doesn't fade away?"

Aadhav leaned in, his eyes earnest. "It starts with understanding. Hindus need to delve into their own *Sanatana Dharma*, to learn about their history, philosophy, and traditions. It's not just about celebrating festivals; it's about understanding the 'why' behind them. Why do we perform rituals? What do our texts say? It's about reclaiming our narrative."

Raj nodded, feeling a sense of urgency. "And how do we do that? It seems overwhelming."

"Start small," Aadhav suggested. "Engage with your community. Attend local cultural events, read about your heritage, and share that knowledge with others. Encourage discussions about our traditions and values. It's about creating a ripple effect. When one person understands, they can inspire others."

Raj smiled, feeling inspired. "I like that idea. It's like planting seeds. If we nurture them, they can grow into something beautiful."

"Exactly!" Aadhav exclaimed; his enthusiasm infectious. "And we must also be vocal about it. When we see cultural misappropriation or misunderstanding, we should speak up. It's not about being defensive; it's about educating others and fostering respect for our traditions."

Raj raised his glass, a newfound determination in his eyes. "To understanding our roots and celebrating our culture!"

Aadhav clinked his glass against Raj's, a smile spreading across his face. "And to being proud of who we are, while embracing the diversity around us. Let's not forget that we can learn from other cultures without losing our own identity."

As they continued their conversation, the bar buzzed with life around them, but Raj and Aadhav were absorbed in their thoughts. They discussed the nuances of identity, the importance of cultural preservation, and the delicate balance between embracing diversity and honoring one's roots.

In that moment, they realized that the journey of understanding one's culture was not just a personal endeavor; it was a collective responsibility. As they left the bar, the cool night air greeted them, a reminder that while the world was vast and varied, the essence of who they were—Hindus with a rich heritage—was something to be cherished and celebrated.

"Let's make a pact," Raj said, his voice resolute. "To actively learn about our culture and share it with others. We owe it to ourselves and future generations."

"Agreed," Aadhav replied, a sense of purpose igniting within him. "Let's be the torchbearers of our *Sanatana Dharma*, ensuring that it continues to thrive in a world that often forgets."

As they walked down the street, the stars twinkling above, they felt a renewed sense of connection—not just to each other, but to their culture, their history, and the vibrant tapestry of life that surrounded them. The conversation had sparked something profound, a commitment to understanding and preserving their identity in a rapidly changing world.

Ignorance to Indoctrination

Gayatri, known to her friends as G, found herself at a crossroads in life, standing in the wreckage of what had once seemed like a promising future. Just a week after her boyfriend walked out, she received the news that her job was gone too. It felt like the universe had conspired against her, leaving her adrift in a sea of despair. The bright lights of her city, once inviting, now felt like a harsh glare, illuminating her failures.

G took to the bottle, her nightly ritual becoming a blur of cheap wine and dimly lit bars. Each sip was a temporary escape, a fleeting moment where the weight of her world felt lighter. But as the alcohol flowed, so did the darkness. Friends reached out, but their words felt hollow, like echoes in a vast canyon. They didn't understand the depth of her pain, nor did they grasp the cultural and spiritual turmoil that had begun to consume her. She looked for answers everywhere – logic, science or religion, but alas, she did not find anything helpful.

One evening, sitting on her friend Riya's couch, G vented her frustrations. "I just don't get it, Riya. Why should I stick to *Sanatana Dharma*? It feels outdated and suffocating."

Riya, her voice calm, replied, "But G, have you really explored it? It's not just rituals; it's a philosophy of life."

"Philosophy? It seems more like a set of rules designed to control us," G snapped, pouring herself another glass of wine.

"Maybe it feels that way because you haven't understood it fully. Ask yourself, what do you think about *karma*?" Riya probed gently.

"I think *karma* is a bitch. Bites us." She spoke and then acknowledges, "Am sorry. I don't know, it's just... what goes around comes around, right? But that doesn't explain why bad things happen to good people," G retorted, frustration bubbling to the surface.

"Exactly! That's a question worth exploring. Why don't we dive into it together?" Riya suggested, her eyes filled with encouragement.

Over the next few days, G and Riya engaged in deep discussions about *Sanatana Dharma*. They sat at coffee shops, surrounded by the aroma of freshly brewed coffee, as Riya asked questions that challenged G's understanding.

"Okay, let's start with *karma*. If it's true, then why do innocent people suffer?" Riya asked, sipping her latte.

G leaned back in her chair, her brow furrowed. "Maybe it's just a way to explain life's unfairness? Like, we can't always control what happens to us."

"But what if it's more about the choices we make? Each action has consequences," Riya countered.

G sighed, "I guess that makes sense, but it feels like a lot of pressure. What if I make the wrong choice?"

"Isn't that part of being human? Learning from mistakes?" Riya replied, her tone gentle yet firm.

G felt the weight of Riya's words but still clung to her skepticism. "I don't know, Riya. It just feels like a lot of blame is placed on individuals."

As their conversations continued, G found herself becoming more quizzical. Each question Riya posed led to another layer of confusion.

"Okay, what about *dharma*? What does it mean to you?" Riya asked one afternoon.

G shrugged, her mind racing. "Isn't it just about duty? But whose duty? And what if I don't want to follow it?"

"Isn't that the point? To find your own path within it?" Riya replied, her eyes sparkling with curiosity.

G frowned, "But how do I know what my path is? What if I'm just wandering aimlessly?"

"Maybe you need to explore that aimlessness. What if it's a part of your journey?" Riya suggested, leaning in.

"Ugh, it's so confusing! Why can't it just be simple?" G exclaimed, frustration creeping in.

As the weeks passed, G's confusion deepened. She felt a void inside her, a chasm that seemed impossible to fill. One evening, she sat on her bed, staring at the wall, when Riya knocked and entered.

"Hey, you okay?" Riya asked, concern etched on her face.

"I feel lost. I'm caught in this endless loop of questions and no answers," G admitted, her voice trembling.

"Maybe that's okay. Maybe you don't need all the answers right now," Riya suggested, sitting beside her.

"But it's exhausting! I thought exploring my beliefs would help, but it's just made me feel worse," G confessed, tears brimming in her eyes.

Riya placed a comforting hand on her shoulder. "It's a process, G. Sometimes you must sit in the discomfort to find clarity."

As G grappled with her confusion, she found herself drawn to the local Scientology center, intrigued by the promise of enlightenment. One afternoon, she visited the center, where they were greeted by a receptionist.

"Welcome! Are you here to learn more about Scientology?" the receptionist asked with a bright smile.

"We are just curious," G replied hesitantly.

"Curiosity is the first step! Let me introduce you to one of our guides," the receptionist said, leading them to a room filled with books and pamphlets.

A charismatic man named David approached them. "I'm glad you're here! Scientology offers answers to the questions you've been wrestling with. What brings you in today?"

G exchanged a glance with Riya, who nodded encouragingly. "I have a lot of questions about life and purpose," G admitted.

"Perfect! Let's start with your beliefs. What do you think about the nature of existence?" David asked, his eyes gleaming with enthusiasm.

G hesitated, "I don't know. I feel like everything is just random chaos."

David leaned in, "That's a common feeling. But what if I told you that life has a purpose? That we can take control of our destinies through understanding?"

G felt a flicker of hope. "How?"

"Through the teachings of Scientology! We believe in the power of the mind and the ability to shape our reality. Let's explore this together," David said, handing her a pamphlet.

As G delved deeper into the teachings of Scientology, she found herself captivated by the promise of self-discovery and empowerment. The process was intoxicating, and she began attending sessions regularly, feeling a sense of belonging she hadn't experienced in a long time.

One evening, after a particularly enlightening session, G turned to Riya. "I think I'm starting to understand. It's like I've been given a new lens to view the world."

Riya frowned, concern creeping into her voice. "But G, what about your own beliefs? What about *Sanatana Dharma*? It is not like you have explored its meaning fully to decide that it does not apply. You are copping out and choosing something totally new. Are you not biased and rejecting your own culture without even knowing anything about it?"

"I don't know, Riya. It just feels so complicated. This is simple, and it makes sense to me," G replied, her voice tinged with excitement.

"But at what cost? Are you not abandoning your roots?" Riya pressed, her worry evident.

G paused, the question hanging in the air. "Maybe I need to let go of what I thought I knew to embrace something new."

Months passed, and the transformation within G was palpable. The alcohol that had once been her refuge was now a distant memory. She replaced her nightly binges with the teachings of Scientology that had once felt foreign. But as she immersed herself in this new ideology, a nagging feeling began to surface—an unsettling sense of disconnection from her heritage.

One evening, as she stood on her balcony, watching the sunset paint the sky in hues of orange and pink, G felt a profound sense of gratitude wash over her. The struggles she had endured were now steppingstones, guiding her toward a deeper understanding of herself and her place in the world. But she also felt a void where her connection to her own culture had once thrived.

When she turned on the TV to watch the movie The Kerala Story, that someone recommended, she realized to her horror that the girls were being indoctrinated in the same way she was. The process was clear. Ask questions, and disparage Hindu *Dharma*, then make the person confused. The next stage is to create a void where the person will accept anything and then inject the new ideology. She had unfortunately gone through the process herself and led herself to be indoctrinated by Scientology. What more it is than an unverifiable belief system that uses new words in modern contexts?

Determined to reconcile her feelings, G sought out Riya once more. They met at their favorite café, the familiar aroma of coffee enveloping them.

"Riya, I've been thinking. I feel like I've replaced one set of beliefs with another, but I'm still not whole," G confessed, her heart racing.

Riya looked at her, a mix of relief and concern in her eyes. "What do you mean?"

"I've been so focused on finding answers outside of myself that I've neglected my own roots. I want to understand *Sanatana Dharma*, not just dismiss it," G admitted, tears welling up. And she explained about the horrors of indoctrination she saw in the movie.

With newfound clarity, G began to explore her spirituality with an open heart. She attended workshops on Hindu philosophy, immersing herself in the teachings that had once felt suffocating. The more she learned, the more she understood the beauty of her heritage—the richness of the stories, the depth of the rituals, and the wisdom embedded in the teachings of *karma* and *dharma*.

G's journey was not without its challenges. There were days when the shadows of her past crept back in, whispering doubts and fears. But she had developed tools to combat those moments—her mantra, her yoga, and her commitment to serving others. Each time she faced a setback, she reminded herself of the principles of *Karma Yoga,* focusing on the actions she could take in the present rather than the burdens of the past.

In the end, G emerged not just as a survivor of her circumstances but as a beacon of hope for others. She began sharing her story, encouraging those who felt lost to reconnect with their roots and explore the transformative power of their own traditions. G had learned that understanding and embracing her own *dharma* was the key to unlocking her potential.

As she stood before a group of eager listeners, sharing the lessons of her journey, G felt a sense of fulfillment that she had once thought impossible. She had taken charge of her life, not by abandoning her past but by embracing it with open arms. The *Gayatri Mantra* echoed in her heart, a reminder that she was not defined by her struggles but by her ability to rise above them, transforming pain into purpose.

Tennis Lessons Anyone?

It was a sunny afternoon in the quiet suburban neighborhood when Lakshmi, a devoted *Hindu* mother, found herself at the doorstep of the local church. Her daughter, Richa, had been invited by her friends to join the free tennis lessons offered by the church, and Lakshmi couldn't resist the opportunity to save some money while providing her daughter with a fun activity. *Desi's* love to save money! No one can resist freebies, can they?

As Lakshmi walked through the church doors, she was greeted by a group of enthusiastic mothers, all eager to share their experiences with the tennis lessons. "It's such a great deal, Lakshmi!" exclaimed Priya, one of Richa's classmates' mothers. "Not only do we get free tennis coaching, but the kids also learn valuable moral lessons from the coach, Alan." Lakshmi nodded politely, but deep down, she couldn't help but feel a sense of unease. As a *Hindu*, she believed in the importance of her own culture and the rich philosophical teachings it offered. The idea of her daughter being exposed to Christian teachings during the tennis lessons didn't sit well with her.

On the first day of the tennis lessons, Lakshmi accompanied Richa to the church courts. As the children began their warm-up exercises, Lakshmi noticed that the coach, Alan, was also a priest in the church. She watched intently as he moved from one child to another, offering guidance and encouragement.

However, as the lesson progressed, Lakshmi's unease grew. Instead of focusing solely on tennis, Alan began to preach about the teachings of Jesus Christ. The two-hour session was split into two halves, strategically. He would teach for 45 minutes and then during the fifteen-minute water break, will lecture the kids, under the pretext of correcting their tennis mistakes. After another 45 minutes, he would complete his moral lessons. He spoke passionately about the importance of faith and the love of God, encouraging the children to embrace these values in their daily lives. Lakshmi's heart sank as she saw the other mothers nodding in agreement, seemingly unaware or unconcerned about the religious undertones of the lessons. Prima-facie it looked all good – he was only teaching them morals. But Lakshmi knew better. This was what she had seen happen to several of her friends as she grew up in India. She knew that she had to decide – should she allow Richa to continue with the lessons, or should she pull her out?

After the lesson, Lakshmi approached Alan and politely expressed her concerns. "Coach Alan," she began, "I appreciate the opportunity you're providing for the children, but I'm worried about the religious aspect of the lessons." Alan looked surprised by her statement. "Religious aspect?" he asked, puzzled. "I'm simply sharing moral lessons that can help the children grow into better individuals." Lakshmi shook her head. "But you're doing it through the lens of Christianity. As a *Hindu*, I believe in the importance of my own culture and the rich philosophical teachings it offers." Alan listened intently as Lakshmi explained her perspective. He understood her concerns and acknowledged that the lessons might be perceived as a form of indoctrination. "I apologize if I've made you uncomfortable," he said sincerely. "My intention was never to impose my beliefs on the children, but rather to share universal values that can help them in their lives." Lakshmi appreciated his honesty and openness to discussion. "I know your intentions are good, Coach Alan," she said. "But I worry that my daughter might grow up hating or not liking her own culture, which offers so much more variety, color, and deeper philosophical meaning to life." She did not mention anything about the proselytization and conversions that she had seen growing up in a small village outskirt of Chennai. The local church, abetted by the Dravidian movement, were in the business of 'collecting souls' for salvation, doling out economic benefits to the underprivileged. Her best friend was now a Christian, with a Hindu name, minus the *bindi* on her forehead and stripped off any traces of her culture.

News of Lakshmi's confrontation with Coach Alan quickly spread among the mothers. Some, like Priya, were quick to defend the lessons. "What's the big deal?" she asked. "The kids are learning valuable life lessons, and it's not like they're being forced to convert to Christianity." Others, like Neha, were more understanding of Lakshmi's perspective. "I can see where you're coming from, Lakshmi," she said. "As Hindus, we should be proud of our own rich spiritual heritage and the wisdom it offers." The debate raged on, with some mothers arguing that the lessons were harmless and that the children could learn from multiple faiths, while others supported Lakshmi's stance that the lessons were a form of subtle indoctrination. Lakshmi listened to the arguments on both sides, but her mind was made up. She knew that she had to stand firm in her beliefs and protect her daughter's spiritual identity. She firmly said – *no*, and walked away. As she walked away she heard one of the mom's say, "There is no free lunch." Lakshmi felt extremely sad at the stupidity of the woman who was offering the mind of a young innocent child to be indoctrinated. *What was the kid's fault if the mother herself did not know anything about her own rich Hindu culture and willing to let go of her child's most fundamental foundation to a rich culture that taught way of life, and not insisting on rigid morals & ethics, unlike the Abrahamic religions?*

When Richa learned of her mother's decision, she was understandably upset. "But Mom, all my friends are there, and Coach Alan is so much fun!" she pleaded. Lakshmi hugged her daughter and explained her reasons. "I know it's hard, sweetheart," she said. "But I want you to grow up proud of your *Hindu* heritage and the beautiful teachings it offers. The lessons at the church, while well-intentioned, might make you feel like your own religion is not good enough." Richa listened intently, and although she didn't fully understand the complexities of the situation, she trusted her mother's judgment. Lakshmi promised to find another tennis coach who could teach Richa without any religious undertones.

In the weeks that followed, Lakshmi's decision to withdraw Richa from the tennis lessons sparked a heated debate among the mothers. Some continued to support her stance, while others remained unconvinced. Lakshmi, however, stood firm in her beliefs. She knew that as a *Hindu* mother, it was her responsibility to ensure that her daughter grew up with a strong sense of spiritual identity and pride in her own faith. Through this experience, Lakshmi learned that sometimes, standing up for one's beliefs can be challenging, but it is necessary to maintain a strong sense of self and to pass on that strength to the next generation. *If parents are working hard to create a strong financially secure future for their children, is it not their responsibility to create a culturally secure future as well?*

One Size Fits All?

In a small town in India, two teenagers, Aryan and Meera, lived parallel lives, unaware of each other's existence. Aryan, a bright boy with a curious mind, was raised in a traditional Hindu household. He often felt suffocated by the rigid structures of his society, particularly the caste system. He believed it was an archaic form of segregation that had no place in modern life. His family practiced Hinduism devoutly, but Aryan found himself questioning the very foundations. Meera, on the other hand, was a spirited girl who loved exploring the world around her. Raised in a similar Hindu environment, she was overwhelmed by the multitude of gods and rituals. Each day brought new questions about why people prayed to different deities and what they sought from them. She often felt lost in the sea of idols and chants that filled her temple visits. As they both navigated their teenage years, their discontent grew. Aryan's frustration with Hinduism deepened as he conflated social evils and equating them to spiritual teachings. He believed that *Yoga* was the essence of *Hinduism* and that it focused solely on physical postures rather than its true purpose: union with the divine. He also struggled with the concept of multiple Gods, viewing them as mere representations for different needs rather than aspects of a singular divine reality. Similarly, Meera's confusion about prayer led her to believe that Hindus prayed for material desires or out of fear rather than seeking a deeper connection with God. And, she couldn't understand why women were often sidelined during their periods and barred entry from temples, which only added to her growing disillusionment.

As they entered adulthood, Aryan and Meera sought solace in alternative beliefs. Aryan discovered Christianity through friends who spoke passionately about Jesus' love for all humanity. The simplicity of the message resonated with him: "Jesus loves you." It was a simple catch-all phrase expressing complex theology in the form of a savior in Jesus. He was also drawn to the idea that one could read the Bible in church rather than the Hindu way of chanting prayers in temples; without understanding their meanings. He saw Christianity as a path free from the complexities he associated with Hinduism. Meanwhile, Meera encountered Islam through a college friend who introduced her to its teachings. Fascinated by the structured nature of Islamic practices, she appreciated how Muslims prayed five times a day and adhered to a clear set of guidelines. The dress code for women seemed empowering to her; it provided dignity and respect in a world where she felt marginalized as a woman in Hindu society. And there was no mention about menstruation.

Over time, both Aryan and Meera embraced their new faiths wholeheartedly. Much to the disdain of their parents.

Aryan's and Meera's decisions to convert to Christianity and Islam respectively were met with shock and disappointment by their parents. They had raised their children in a loving Hindu household, instilling in them the values of their faith. However, they realized too late that they had failed to adequately address their children's questions and doubts about Hinduism. Aryan's parents were particularly distressed by his rejection of the caste system, which they saw as an evil social construct propagated by some who misinterpreted the spiritual teachings for selfish benefits. They tried to explain the deeper meaning behind the categorization of people based on their mindset and actions, but Aryan remained unconvinced. His father guiltily lamented, "We should have taken the time to help you understand the true essence of Hinduism, beyond the superficial aspects." Meera's mother, on the other hand, was saddened by her daughter's confusion about the multiple deities and the purpose of prayer. She was in tears when Meera decided she will not perform *Kathak* dance anymore as such performances were not allowed in Islam. Her mother attempted to clarify that the various gods and goddesses were manifestations of the one divine, each representing different aspects of the Supreme Being. "*Mukti* is important, and different *murtis* are just a way. Don't stick to the *murtis*." She spoke to her, but it was already too late. Her explanations fell short, leaving Meera still perplexed.

Both sets of parents grappled with the guilt of not providing their children with a more comprehensive understanding of Hinduism. They realized that their own lack of knowledge and inability to address their children's queries had contributed to their misguided perceptions. As Aryan's mother confessed, "We assumed that by immersing you in our traditions, you would naturally understand their deeper meanings. But we failed to recognize your need for deeper explanations."

Years passed as Aryan and Meera immersed themselves in their respective new faiths. They had moved to the US to pursue their careers. And they both enjoyed the lifestyle here – innumerable choices for anything and everything – right from simple choices like food, drink or how to commute to complicated choices like whom to date, where to stay etc. They had also taken advantage of the individualistic lifestyle that US society promotes, unlike the restrictive small-town culture they had grown up back in India.

Aryan often debated with friends about Hinduism's perceived flaws, focusing on what he considered its outdated practices and beliefs. He dismissed any notion that Krishna or Vishnu could embody strength or masculinity; to him, they seemed effeminate compared to the powerful image he held of Jesus. Meera continued her exploration of Islam while grappling with her past misunderstandings about Hinduism. She often found herself defending her new beliefs against those who criticized Islam.

Despite their separate journeys, both Aryan and Meera occasionally reflected on their childhood beliefs—though they did so with disdain rather than curiosity. There were times when they felt they may have made a hasty choice, only to brush that thought soon enough, lest the emotions clouded their intellect and made them depressed.

One fateful day, ten years after they had chosen their paths, Aryan boarded an Amtrak train bound for New York City for a conference. As fate would have it, Meera was on the same train heading to visit a friend. As they settled into their seats across from each other, neither recognized the other until a chance glance revealed familiarity. They did not know well enough of each other while growing up but word of mouth had reached about each other. They never made attempts to meet up here in the US. Parallel tracks they were.

They exchanged hesitant smiles before launching into conversation.

"What brings you here?" Aryan asked casually.

"I'm visiting a friend," Meera replied. "And you?"

"Going to a conference," he said.

It was liberating to speak with a near stranger and express one's views freely. Their conversation flowed naturally as they discussed their lives over the past decade—their newfound faiths, experiences, and challenges. However, as they spoke about their respective beliefs, old misunderstandings began to surface.

"I never understood why people pray to so many gods in Hinduism," Meera said thoughtfully. "It seems like you're just asking for things instead of connecting with God." Aryan nodded vigorously.

"Exactly! And don't get me started on how women are treated during their periods! It's absurd!" Meera frowned.

Hours passed as they shared stories about their experiences within Christianity and Islam. Aryan spoke passionately about how Jesus taught love without judgment while lamenting what he perceived as Hinduism's rigid structures.

"Christianity is all about acceptance," he said earnestly. "We don't have caste systems or complicated rituals."

A few moments of silence swooped them both. Then Meera spoke slowly.

"Unlike you, I do have some misgivings at times that I push away into a corner of the mind."

Aryan listened intently and asked her to tell him more.

"Well, it just seems that there is a rigidity. After the initial euphoria of a few weeks, the rigidity seems to weigh down on me. The fear of hell starts to play on my mind. "

She continued sharing her own struggles with misconceptions surrounding Islam.

"Although I willingly gave up *Kathak,* I am not so sure if that is the right thing." Meera had always been fascinated by the concept of the body as a vehicle for expressing love and devotion to the divine. She had participated in various Hindu festivals and rituals that involved song, dance, and other forms of artistic expression. The idea of covering up and restricting the body, as required by the hijab, seemed to go against her understanding of the body as an instrument for spiritual connection. She did not wear one here in the US.

"I too at times had certain misgivings. I still do, but I don't think I have the answers. This path I am following seems easy to follow, uncomplicated. But I admit, I probably adopted to this path without having understood the nuances of Hinduism." He too admitted.

As night fell outside the train window, Aryan and Meera continued discussing their journeys—each revelation peeling back layers of misunderstanding built over years.

They were suddenly interrupted by a tall, gentle man with kind eyes and a flowing beard. He was wearing jeans and an orange *kurta* that resembled what the *sannyasis* wore generally. He was getting off a station in between and spoke with them.

"Sorry, I overheard what you were talking about and wanted to ask you to reflect on this. Your life in US seems to be filled with taking pride in choices you have and ability to experiment and decide. I also gathered that you both seemed to have enjoyed the individualistic pursuits and lifestyle that US offers. And, this place is the place that promotes rational thinking. Did you ever consider if Hinduism – that you both left to pursue other paths, ever offered that choice? Do your current paths offer any choice at all? How would you like a path that offered innumerable choices to people with different mindsets? Does 'one size fits all' approach ever work in life? If not, then why should it work in a spiritual path too? We are individuals first, each with a different mindset and it would be tough to follow a path of masses, unless it is customized for our mindset. How rational are your current paths? Have they satisfied your logical questions? For example, have you ever wondered why Hindus worship everyone & everything around? That's because we don't say – there is only one God; but truly we say – there is only God. And different traditions, cultures and customs are adaptations for different types of mindsets. It's as simple as that." He added as walked away clutching his small bag but left the gentle smile behind and those piercing eyes that communicated to the hearts to churn and the mind to think critically. "There is no proselytization, nor apostasy is a crime. *Sanatana Dharma*[29] is an eternal religion, whose principle can be summarized in one word – *ahimsa*.

They would later see him on TV presenting about Hindu philosophy and learnt that he was the famous Swami Viveka Ananda of the Ramakrishna order.

"I think we both missed something important. What that person said makes sense. We chose simplicity and rigidity and became victims of orthodoxy and mass-belief." Aryan mused softly. His misgivings were gaining attention, pressing down the hubris he had built up so far about his new path.

"What do you mean?" Meera asked.

"We forgot that every path has its beauty," he replied thoughtfully. "And we allowed our misunderstandings to cloud our perceptions. Maybe we should have first critically examined the contradictions in Hinduism before choosing an alternate path." She could not disagree. *It feels like the advice I gave to Reena. When Reena was dumped by her boyfriend, I had advised her to marry the next guy who was interested in her, just to spite her ex-boyfriend! How stupid was that!* She thought.

---

29   अद्रोह: सर्वभूतेषु कर्मणा मनसा गिरा ।
       अनुग्रहश्च दानं च सतां धर्म: सनातन: ॥
       adroha: sarvabhūteṣu karmaṇā manasā girā |
       anugrahaśca dānaṃ ca satāṃ dharma: sanātana: ||
       Abstention from injury, as regards all creatures in thought, word and deed, kindness and charity, are the eternal (*Sanatana*) duties (*dharma*) of those who are good.

As dawn approached outside the train window—a new day dawning—they realized how much they had grown through this unexpected encounter.

The train finally pulled into New York City after an enlightening journey together—one filled with laughter, tears, and revelations about faith and identity. Before parting ways at the station, Aryan turned to Meera with newfound sincerity in his eyes.

"You know… I think we should explore our roots again."

"Together?" she asked hesitantly yet hopefully. She was not sure of wading through the complexities of Hinduism.

"Why not?" he smiled warmly. Secretly he was relieved to find a partner navigate the confusions.

Over the next year, Aryan and Meera embarked on a journey back into Hinduism together—visiting temples, reading scriptures, and engaging with spiritual leaders who helped them reconnect with their heritage. They discovered Vedanta, explaining the philosophy behind the outer layers of customs, traditions, rituals. They discovered profound truths within Hindu philosophy—the importance of *dharma, karma* and *moksha*. Their understanding deepened as they embraced not only their individual identities but also each other's perspectives along this path toward rediscovery. As time passed and love blossomed between them amidst shared experiences rooted in spirituality—they decided to marry.

On a beautiful spring day surrounded by family and friends at a serene temple adorned with flowers—a symbol of rebirth—the couple exchanged vows steeped in Hindu tradition yet infused with modern understanding.

Body Building & Protein Sankat

Disgust churned in his stomach, a stark contrast to the juicy burger he devoured a few hours ago. The visit to the slaughterhouse, a dare from his friends, had shattered his comfortable ignorance. He couldn't unsee the terror in those bovine eyes.

Sid stared at the grotesque scene before him – rows of cows crammed into metal cages, their moos echoing a symphony of despair. One look at their beautiful eyes, he could imagine them begging everyone to let them free. Not to be bound and treated like cattle, and subsequently as food. Those eyes were pleading everyone to treat them as living beings. Then he saw a few more cows being led by someone into a room full of meat lying on the floor to its final transition from a living being to piece of meat. He wasn't sure but he also probably imagined the meat strewn on the floor mixed with urine, dung and mud from the hooves of the animals being led for slaughter.

He saw a special machine, made of solid metal that enveloped the animal completely except for its neck and head. Like a CAT scan machine in a hospital. Then he saw a smooth metal piece slowly making its way from the bottom of the neck to the top, stretching the neck backwards and holding it tight. He saw the entire machine rotate 180 degrees, and the animal was being made to do a deliberate *shirsasana*.

Almost. He could not look beyond. Perhaps there was a sharp blade at the bottom that slit the throat instantly. Or maybe, it bled the animal to death. He did not care.

All he could see was those pitiable eyes. For two nights he had not slept well after realizing how the juicy burger he ate all started out as.

"What I eat is just food. It is nourishment for me. I don't care how it is made." He had declared two days ago biting the juicy burger. This was the turning point in his life.

"Oh no. It is convenient for anyone to buy meat off the supermarket shelves, like buying vegetables. But not so easy to look at how it is made and still enjoy the burger." Spoke one of his close friends, who had recently become a vegan.

His friend was challenging his thinking, like friends usually do. Afterall, what do twenty – to twenty-five-year-olds talk about when they meet? Work, dating, food, wine, treks, reminiscing about dorm days….and today was the day for food choices. California was home to all sorts of diets. Vegetarianism, paleo, raw, vegan, all meat and so on. It was indeed pro-choice, although that term has been usurped by the pro-abortion campaigners.

Sometimes some conversations have a lasting impact. This one was for Sid.

After what he saw at the slaughterhouse, he did not feel like visiting the butcher stall to complete his tour. What difference does it make to know how anyone is handling a dead body? There is no difference between a timber store or a butcher shop after that.

Sid's decision was made – vegetarianism it was.

But soon, a new challenge arose. Sid, always athletic, had recently taken up bodybuilding, aiming for a sculpted physique. Protein, his trainer emphasized, was the holy grail of muscle growth. The thought of tofu scrambling every morning instead of a hearty sausage omelet left him feeling deflated.

Was he giving up his dream body for a moral stand?

Days turned into weeks, filled with internal conflict. Scouring the internet for vegetarian bodybuilding options, Sid felt overwhelmed. Pea protein shakes, lentil curries – none held the same appeal as a juicy steak. And he had to consume a whole lot more in quantity to meet the same protein needs a meat burger would have given him.

Dejected, he sat on a park bench, watching kids play. A group of girls giggled, their eyes lingering on a group of boys flexing their muscles. A pang of longing shot through him. Maybe the trainer was right. Maybe meat was the key.

Suddenly, a voice broke him out of his reverie. "Looking glum, champ," said an old man, his eyes twinkling despite the wrinkles etched on his face. He had regularly seen this person, always waving at him as Sid was getting his intense running practice in the park. He always supplemented cardio to pumping iron at the gym.

They had never spoken to each other, but both had a certain familiarity, which did not make them strangers to each other. Yet, just strange park buddies. He made him talk. Sid poured out his heart, the protein struggle, the bodybuilding dream.

The old man chuckled. "Why do you want those muscles?"

Sid hesitated. "Well, to look good, I guess. Maybe impress…" he trailed off, a flicker of embarrassment crossing his face.

The old man smiled knowingly. "Impress who? Those fleeting glances from girls? True strength comes from within. It's about discipline, perseverance, and pushing your limits. Not about chasing fleeting validation."

Sid's heart pounded. The old man's words resonated deep within. He wasn't building a body; he was building a fragile ego, dependent on the fleeting approval of others.

That day, Sid made a new choice. He wouldn't abandon his fitness goals, but he would redefine them. He delved deeper into bodyweight exercises, yoga for flexibility, calisthenics and a balanced vegetarian diet. The initial days were tough, but his resolve grew stronger with every bead of sweat. He discovered a different kind of strength – the strength of conviction, the power of self-belief.

Slowly, his body changed. He became leaner, stronger, with a newfound resilience. More importantly, he gained a sense of peace that no amount of protein could ever provide. He understood that true strength wasn't about sculpted muscles; it was about aligning your actions with your beliefs and finding validation from within. And that was the most powerful physique he could ever achieve.

Reframing Sanatana Dharma for a Modern Mind

1. *Sanatana* – eternal; *Dharma* – laws of nature. 'Hinduism' is the popular alternate name for this path, although the word *Hindu* is of recent Persian origin (circa 1500 AD). It is a way of living in harmony with the universe.

2. It is NOT a 'religion' in the strictest definition of word because it is **not** a 'belief' system. You don't have to accept anything as true if you don't see the logic. It does NOT expect you to have any 'faith' in someone or something, other than your own intelligence, open to inquiry and rational thinking. It expects you to learn the philosophy/theology as if you were learning any scientific subject.

3. Eternal laws are eternal, some in the realm of observable universe and some beyond. They are facts. Some easily visible to all (e.g. gravity), some discovered by scientists (e.g. magnetism) and some that are not easily visible or provable by scientific methods, like law of *karma*. These laws explain:

    a. nature of this universe *including* human mind (not just earth, space).

    b. if this universe was 'created' or not by any being, and if created, who is creator?

    c.   what is *my* relationship with that creator? Why should I care?

    d.   what is *my* relationship with this universe? Why should I care?

4.   No one 'said' or 'wrote down' these laws of nature. It is not a book either. These laws are simply called *Vedas* – meaning **knowledge (or *that which must be known*)** in *Sanskrit* language. So, there are no '*books*' per se! However, one of the *Rishis*, called *Veda Vyasa* categorized them into four *Vedas* – *Rg, Yajur, Sama, Atharvana Vedas*. There are several other sub-categories of *knowledge* to explain *Vedas* better to different types of minds – called *Vedangas, Itihasas, Puranas. Ramayana & Mahabharata* are two *puranas*. *Vedas* cannot be equated to Bible or Koran, which are books written.

5.   *Rishis* who discovered these eternal laws, communicated these orally and students understood, memorized and propagated with the *sole intention* of explaining how a human life must be lived in harmony with the universe. By learning about eternal laws, humans can determine how best to use them and live in synch with this universe. When understood this way, *Vedas* are not mere utterances but a means of knowledge to know what is not available for discovery through our limited senses.

6.   Human goals are broadly in four categories: (a) freedom from insecurity (*artha*), (b) obtaining what is desirable (*kama*), (c) freedom from all suffering due to insecurities, desires & be content at all times/places (*moksha*), (d) with 'ethically' right behavior (*dharma*).

7. To explain the observed differences in human conditions and the different goals humans strive for, *karma* theory and *rebirth* theory are posited. You can choose to believe these or not with as much conviction as you would choose to believe the big-bang theory, or theory of evolution.

8. Human beings go through four psychological stages of maturity over age:
    a. learning how life needs to be lived, not just to earn (*brahmacharya*)
    b. earning /spending /contributing to society and supporting society (*grhasta*)
    c. reflecting on purpose of their life, after being socially active and contributing to society (*vanaprastha*)
    d. working actively to realize the true purpose of their life (*sannyasa*).

    The emphasis of stage is explained in *Vedas*.

9. The philosophy /theology does not say that the ultimate human purpose is to go to 'heaven' or avoid 'hell'. These are Abrahamic theology constructs and definition of *svarga*, *naraka* are not the same as heaven, hell respectively.

10. Reason why we should understand the *Vedas* is: They explain, what one should do in each life stage, how they should do it, what benefits will they get in life, by implementing the understanding of *Vedas*. The goal of *Vedas* is to show the path for being content at all times/ places (*moksha*)

11. There are four concentric circles to understand any culture. Outer to innermost core layer are:

<table>
<tr><td>a.</td><td>Cultural /Visible layer</td><td>:</td><td>e.g. festivals, clothing, symbols (eg. bindi)</td></tr>
<tr><td>b.</td><td>Devotional layer</td><td>:</td><td>e.g. temples, god, puja, bhajan</td></tr>
<tr><td>c.</td><td>Ritual layer</td><td>:</td><td>e.g. homa, sraddha, namakarana, weddings</td></tr>
<tr><td>d.</td><td>Philosophical/ theology layer</td><td>:</td><td>e.g. Vedanta, Mimamsa, Nyaya</td></tr>
</table>

12. The philosophical layer is essential to understand the purpose and significance of various other layers. If one does not understand the underlying philosophy, the other cultural elements seem meaningless.

Basic Tenets of Sanatana Dharma

1. Intelligent universe (earth in its orbit, object dropped always falls….) must have an intelligence behind it. *Vedas* hypothesize a Creator. Intelligent universe must have come from some raw material (like gold ornament from gold, which in turn comes from earth). To avoid infinite regression problem, *Vedas* hypothesize that raw material <u>also</u> as the Creator itself. So, this intelligent universe has come <u>from</u> a Creator & who has permeated <u>in and every object, place, time, and living being.</u> Therefore, the universe & its Creator cannot be different from each other. This is called intelligence (*chit*) – existence (*sat*) – infinite (*ananda/ananta*), also known as *sat-chit-ananda* (words rearranged). The Creator as defined here is NOT the same as Abrahamic God (Father, Jesus, Holy Spirit or Allah).

2. We notice that nothing is ever created or destroyed in this world. Only transformation happens. This is true even for all living beings. As we grow up from a baby to a teen to adult to old man, the body/mind grows/matures, but 'I' remains the same. So, when we die, the body decomposes, but mind finds another suitable body to go towards the goal of human life, *moksa*. This is called rebirth /reincarnation theory.

3. What type of future body the mind will get depends on how they have lived their past lives, with /without

right behavior (*dharma*). This is called *karma* (*phala*) theory. This indicates that the right circumstances will be created by the Creator for you to fructify your past actions.

4. The intelligent Creator provides each being born with the right body, right environment to progress towards the goal of human life. (So, Creator is also called *karma-phala dhata*, giver of the circumstances & tools we need to fructify our *karmas* done.)

5. Humans know we exist (*sat*), are intelligent (*chit*) but experience sporadic and 'limited' contentment, joy, and happiness. Consequently, we are always searching for that limitlessness in everything – health, wealth, fame, power, intelligence, strength, life span etc.…...

6. When a human being clearly and unambiguously understands the goal of life, the being will have reached a state of no suffering, under any circumstances, always, <u>here & now.</u> Then they will have understood this equivalency of Human (*jiva*) ⇔Universe (*jagat*) ⇔ Intelligent Infinite Creator/Created (*sat-chit-ananda*).

7. To accelerate the human being reach their goal, *Vedas* recommends we develop several values. These are preparatory stages of the mind to understand the nature of Reality as our very own true self. Some of the key values are *ahimsa* (least violence, not non-violence), *satyam* (stating truth, as it is; not as you perceive), *akrodhah* (not being angered), *tyaga* (sharing), *shanti* (peaceful contented mind), *kshanti* (forgiving nature).

Questions/Myths about Sanatana Dharma

1. I do not believe in theories of intelligent creation, rebirth, *karma*. Am I not a *Hindu?* Can you convince me about the validity of your theories?

   The choice to believe any theory is yours. Nobody will convince you. Approach these not as a dogma or belief, but a useful framework. If it helps to explain what you observe, use it. Else don't use it. You are a *Sanatani* (or a *Hindu)* irrespective of the choice you make.

2. I am an atheist. I do not believe in 'God'. You use other words – Intelligent creator, *sat-chit-ananda.* Does God exist in *Sanatana-dharma?* Can atheists follow *Sanatana Dharma?*

   Yes, atheists can follow this path. It helps to arrive at unambiguous definitions of the words – atheist, God, Nature, Universe – before deciding answers to these questions. Almost always atheists seem to have an Abrahamic definition for 'God' and are trying to understand this path from that perspective. We don't subscribe to those definitions.

3. **I see that there are literally thousands of forms of 'Gods' that Hindus worship. Who are they? What purpose do the Gods /temples serve? Why should we worship? What exactly is worship? Who exactly am I worshipping?**

    Since in this path, the Creator (known as *Isvara)* is non-distinct to the Universe created, any form can be worshipped. Irrespective of what visible/perceivable symbol is worshipped, you are worshipping *Isvara.* Different forms are used by different people, because the form must resonate with their mindset, and they should feel an affinity. Some popular forms are that of Vishnu, Krishna, Lakshmi, Ganesha, the symbol Om etc. This path says anyone can worship *Isvara* anytime, anywhere, anyhow, and temple visits are not mandatory.

    Worship, known as *puja* is a way of reducing the dissonance in our mind to know our true identity as identical to the Creator.

4. **Is idol-worship important /required in *Sanatana Dharma*. I do not believe in idol-worship. Can I still follow this path?**

    Idol worship is not important or required.

5. **I have heard so much about caste system in Hinduism. Are you avoiding this topic? What is caste system? Are people discriminated in *Sanatana Dharma*? If so, why?**

    Caste is a derivative word from Portuguese, who segregated the society based on European society segregation. In *Sanatana Dharma,* humans are segregated based on their predominant mental qualities (*guna*) and natural affinity to the type of job they would take up (*karma*). This is called *Varna* system. It exists naturally wherever humans are. In the name of 'caste' the society has been wrongly segregated based on birth during the colonial period. This is a social evil that continues even today, that must be called out and eradicated. *Varna* system is NOT based on birth. Neither is it unique to Indian civilization. It is present everywhere.

6. **I have heard of heaven (*svarga*) and hell (*naraka*). What are they? Are they different from Christian ideas of heaven/hell and *jannat /jahannam* of Islam? If so, how? Why should I believe in the *Sanatana Dharma* idea of *svarga & naraka?***

The Abrahamic theologies are completely different. *Sanatana Dharma* first openly proclaims that *svarga, naraka* are NOT the aspirations to obtain/avoid. These are not ultimate goals at all. They are not physical places in space-time. At best one can think of these as mental states of humans. You don't have to believe in these concepts. However, they are a helpful framework to understand *karma & rebirth* theories.

7. **I have heard that killing animals, eating meat is violence. Are Sanatana Dharma followers prohibited from eating meat, flesh? Is everyone expected to be a vegetarian? Isn't eating plants, seeds also violence because they also are life?**

This kind of thinking stems from the misinterpretation of the value of *ahimsa*. *Dharma* are eternal laws in nature. In nature we see the reality of food chain, then isn't it foolish to assume that eating meat is outside of the laws of nature? That is why it should be interpreted as 'less violence' instead of 'non-violence'. Eating plants/seeds is the least violent activity. On enquiry it becomes easy to understand that *ahimsa* is not an absolute value but is dependent on circumstances and intelligent application of the value in practical life situations.

8. **I have heard that women are treated lowly in Sanatana Dharma. If true, why so? If not, explain.**

How can a theology that is based on the principle that the Creator is the Created treat women lowly? That would be going against the very philosophy. On the contrary, women are accorded much more importance and are considered as torch bearers of culture propagation within a family. In the distant past, ancient civilizations had a clear division of labor of work within a family unit. But as societal structure changes, blurring the nature of work itself, women have started working outside of home. A culture that is 'way of life' cannot restrict anyone doing what they want to do.

9. **Does *Sanatana Dharma* proselytize and convert people of other religions? If not, why not? What is the punishment for apostasy?**

There is no proselytization in this path. This is because we don't believe in the concept of heaven, hell as the final goal of a human. Abrahamic religions have a different theology and are proselytizing religions based on their fundamental belief in heaven, hell after death. There is no punishment for apostasy in Sanatana Dharma. You are free to criticize, debate about the tenets of *Sanatana Dharma*.

10. **Did *Ramayana & Mahabharata* happen? What is the evidence for this?**

They are called *iti* (thus) *hasa* (happened). Hence, they are true incidents in the past. However, there may have been certain writing liberties exercised to explain the theology of *Sanatana Dharma* in a story form, based on these historic incidents. No one will give evidence for the veracity of this claim because the focus of these stories is to teach the theology, and not an authentic narration of history.

11. **Does *Bhagavad Gita* encourage people to wage war? I thought *Sanatana Dharma* promotes *ahimsa* (non-violence) and war is violent. Why?**

No. *Gita* encourages people to fight for *establishing & protecting dharma*.

12. **Did *Sanatana dharma* originate in India? If it is eternal, it should be applicable in all continents., isn't it?**

Yes, this path originated in the geographical region that we know today as India. Yes, it is applicable to all and in all continents. Moreover, even if one does not follow *Sanskrit* or *Vedas* or *Gita*, if they follow the same philosophy, we will call them *Sanatanis*.

13. **Is Aryan invasion theory, correct? Did *Sanatana Dharma* come to India from Europe? I see a lot of similarities between European languages and *Sanskrit*. Was *Sanskrit* a language that originated in Europe and spread to India?**

We don't believe Aryan invasion or migration theories. It is a false Western narrative.

14. **What are the key differences between *Sanatana Dharma* and Christianity, and Islam?**

The basic theology and even definition of essential terms to understand the theology are different. The goals are different. One essential difference is that the *Sanatana Dharma* core principles are simply eternal laws of nature. **However,** the form and practice of how these core principles will reflect in traditions, customs, rituals will change from time to time. This is the reason why we call it as 'way of life'. In this path, living the natural way and adapting the principles into our individual life, based on our individual circumstances, is religious life, and we don't need to change our lifestyle to fit the written word of the religion. For example, there was a time when meat eating was common amongst all. However, as Buddhism developed, the concept of *ahimsa* was extended to animal life as well and incorporated into daily life.

15. **I like what you explained. I want to understand more. What should I read /listen /do next? Should I read *Bhagavad Gita* or *Ramayana* or *Mahabharata*? How**

much time (in hours) I should spend to be confident that I have understood this path – 1 hour, 100 hours, 10,000 hours…??

We recommend you spend atleast 300 hours to understand the concepts and gain a firm footing of the theology. We recommend you watch YouTube videos or listen to podcasts. In this tradition, learning from a qualified teacher is a better way than self-learning. In the words of Swami Dayananda, we believe in tuition and not intuition. A good starting video playlist is by Swami Dayananda Saraswati of Arsha Vidya: https://m.youtube.com/playlist?list=PL7cUdKMzM9J73J3gLoY_FJgdSJmjoZyK0. This "Spiritual Heritage of India Series" has 52 videos, approximately half hour each (total 25 hours approximately). You will surely be able to find supplemental videos to enhance your understanding after you have gone through this playlist.

www.ingramcontent.com/pod-product-compliance
Lightning Source LLC
Chambersburg PA
CBHW031532150726
47990CB00001B/144